NOT THAT KIND OF GIRL

SIOBHAN VIVIAN

ONE PLACE. MANY STORIES

This novel is entirely a work of fiction. The names, characters
and incidents portrayed in it are the work of the author's
imagination. Any resemblance to actual persons, living or
dead, events or localities is entirely coincidental.

HQ
An imprint of HarperCollins*Publishers* Ltd.
1 London Bridge Street
London SE1 9GF

This paperback edition 2017

1
First published in Great Britain by
HQ, an imprint of HarperCollins*Publishers* Ltd. 2017

A catalogue record for this book is
available from the British Library

ISBN: 978-1-84845-697-6

Printed and bound by
CPI Group (UK) Ltd, Croydon, CR0 4YY

Our policy is to use papers that are natural, renewable and
recyclable products and made from wood grown in sustainable
forests. The logging and manufacturing processes conform to
the legal environmental regulations of the country of origin.

Find out more about HarperCollins and the environment at
www.harpercollins.co.uk/green
TM

"It is not often that
someone comes
along who is a
true friend and
a good writer."

– E. B. White

TO MY GIRL, JENNY HAN

PROLOGUE

On the first day of my senior year, I happened to walk past the auditorium during the freshman orientation assembly. One of the two heavy oak doors, each with the Ross Academy crest inset in stained glass, had been propped open. There were only enough students inside to occupy the first few rows of stiff, uncomfortable seats, and the emptiness gave the place a hollow sound that surely made the freshmen feel even smaller and more overwhelmed. I had a free period and a hall pass, so I ducked inside, for old time's sake.

It took all of three minutes before I wanted to scream.

Freshman orientation is a colossal waste of time. Or at least, the way our school handles it, forcing new students to sit through a word-for-word recitation of the *Ross Academy Handbook*, performed in a monotone by the guidance counselor nearest to death. There weren't many *do*s in the *Ross Academy Handbook*. It was pretty much a recitation of *don't*s, from *Don't use your phones during school hours* to *Don't run at an inappropriate pace in the hallways*. More than half the students struggled to stay awake, while the rest focused on subtly and not-so-subtly checking each other out.

If it were up to me, things would be run a lot differently.

First off, I'd split up freshman orientation by gender. For boys, there'd be a simple presentation, done in ten minutes tops. In fact, I could probably cancel their assembly altogether and just hand out a memo. Because there were only three things that added up to a successful high school experience for guys: doing your homework, wearing a condom (if you were so lucky), and deodorizing your leather school shoes every night, because foot sweat plus polyester dress socks makes for unbelievably rank conditions.

Obviously, things would be more involved for the girls.

I'd run their orientation like those *scare 'em straight* drunk-driving lectures, where the police department parks a mangled, twisted car on the front lawn of school, and a guest speaker cries about how he accidentally killed his best friend on the way home from a party. Except instead of the danger of drunk driving, I'd have a speaker talk firsthand about the danger of high school boys.

I know one girl who'd be perfect. She was in my class freshman year. She was nice. Friendly, even to weird kids. Popular, but not enough to make someone jealous, and pretty in a way that was easily overlooked. A few weeks after starting high school, she hit social pay dirt. She found herself a boyfriend.

Chad Rivington stood almost twice her height — an intimidating size until you watched him tuck himself into his rusted baby-blue VW bug, which he loved even as it fell apart. He was a senior with decent grades, nice teeth, and a spot on the varsity basketball team. In other words, he was a catch for a girl of any grade, but especially for a freshman.

They met in the nurse's office — her with a migraine, him brandishing a savage paper cut with the hope of escaping Spanish II. By the end of the week, they were a couple. By the end of the month, they were *the* couple.

They fooled around, of course. But she took things slow, preferring sweet kisses while walking through piles of crispy autumn leaves over half-naked wrestling matches in Chad's cramped backseat.

On their two-month anniversary, Chad asked her to sneak out of Algebra and meet him in the boys' locker room for a secret celebration. The girl had never done anything like that before, but it seemed a fun and exciting dare. Though they hadn't said *I love you* yet, she felt it every time Chad laced their fingers together. Just a week before, after drinking her first three beers at a house party, she'd almost let it slip. But she decided to save it for a special occasion. Like a two-month anniversary.

After glancing over her shoulder, the girl slid inside the boys' locker room and tiptoed down to the very last row of lockers. Chad greeted her with a grin. A moment later, before they'd even said hello, they were kissing. Which quickly turned into groping. It seemed as if her private school uniform had been tailored for this sort of rushed encounter.

He had his hands all over her.

All over her.

And for the first time in their relationship, she didn't worry about where they would go. It was romantic and sexy, and everything inside her melted. Chad had more experience with these sorts of things, and she finally let herself enjoy that.

They might have gone all the way if they'd been in Chad's bedroom, or even in the VW. But they weren't near a bed or a backseat. They were in a stinky locker room, next to a fifth-period gym class. And with every shout for a pass, trill of the whistle, or raucous cheer that leaked in, the danger of being discovered fanned the fog from the girl's good judgment.

"I can't," she said suddenly.

Not there.

Not then.

Chad tried to convince her with words, with kisses. But now she was the opposite of melting. She pulled away from Chad's mouth and said she'd better get back to class.

Chad sagged with disappointment — a familiar posture from their last few dates, though somehow weightier in this instance. He pleaded with her to stay. After all, she'd barely touched him, and he was so turned on. It was only fair to finish what they'd started, right?

She insisted she had to get back to Algebra. Sweetly. Apologetically. And when she noticed how bummed Chad continued to look, she leaned in to kiss him. A cute peck aimed for the tip of his nose, to make it all okay. She felt three words float up her throat, ready at last to be said.

Except Chad turned his head.

The girl felt bad as she hurried back to class. She felt even worse after school, when she came upon some guys razzing Chad next to the smokers' tree. He walked toward his car without so much as a head nod in her direction.

The girl didn't know that Chad's inability to get off with a freshman had become a running joke. A social liability. Even Chad himself had made light of it for weeks, thinking his friends might ease up if he played along. So he'd complain of blue balls after he'd drive her home, or hump his locker door in mock frustration after the girl hugged him good morning before homeroom. Things like that. But Chad's participation only made the others' comments seem more welcome. The teasing became less funny and more personal.

It was one of Chad's friends who suggested the locker-room make-out session. "Use the anniversary," the guy urged. "It's foolproof." It seemed to Chad like everyone in school had their eyes on the clock during fifth period. Everyone expected him to finally get some. And when he came up short, Chad settled on an excuse that would let him entirely off the hook.

When the girl got to school the next morning, whispers hissed like poison arrows aimed at her back. Boys who'd been nice to her at parties, senior girls who'd just started to warm up to her infiltration of their group, now seemed cold and dismissive. Even some of her own classmates, the ones she'd helped usher into the exclusive upper-classmen world, suddenly looked down on her. She couldn't understand it. At least not until she saw Chad and he guiltily headed in the wrong direction so he wouldn't have to talk to her.

After homeroom, the sniffing started. Someone would do it whenever she walked by. She didn't think much of it. It was the height of cold season. But it kept happening. Sniff sniff sniff. Everywhere she went.

It wasn't until lunch, when one of Chad's friends commandeered the white board and named the fish stick entrée after her, that she figured it out.

She just grossed me out too much, she could imagine Chad saying. *I almost gagged, she smelled so bad.* So stupid. So thoughtless. So untrue. But that was all it took. It was over. They were over. She was over.

The initial wave of teasing tapered off after a few months, like any stupid catchphrase or slogan. Chad never apologized. Maybe he cleared his conscience by admitting to someone that it was only a dumb joke, but he said nothing to the girl. And someone else took the baton that spring, when a junior supposedly had a three-way in her parents' shower with two of Chad's teammates.

But the girl, it changed her. The way she walked.

How often she raised her hand in class. What she'd dare to put on her plate at lunch. She was never the same girl again. Not really.

She was Fish Sticks.

This was why trusting boys was just like drinking and driving. Sure, some people took the risk. One or two beers never feels dangerous at the time. And not everyone who drinks and drives gets into an accident.

But to me, it was obvious: Why would you even take the chance?

So, yeah. Orientation should be something more like that. We could provide something useful, instead of policies on locker maintenance. Hearing a story like that was just as important as knowing your blood type, or if you're allergic to bee stings. It was information that could save a girl's life.

CHAPTER ONE

It was the start of our senior year, and my best friend Autumn was feeling nostalgic. She took pictures when we picked up our schedules from the guidance office for the very last time, called it divine intervention that even though we had only two periods in common, the rest were still close enough that we could always walk together. She reminisced about junior year as if it had been decades ago.

Even the state of my appearance after swim class — wet hair hanging like long brown icicles, melting pool water onto my navy cardigan — could make her wistful.

"You smell like summer," she said, resting her head on my shoulder. "I wish it was still summer."

I turned and sniffed my cardigan. Though I'd had it dry-cleaned right before school started, it already reeked of tangy chlorine, so I peeled it off and tied it around my waist. Coach Fallon never sent us to the locker room with enough time to shower. He'd rather us suffer one more lap of butterfly than have thirty seconds to shampoo. Autumn was so lucky that she hurt her shoulder a few years back and had a doctor's note to keep her out of the pool. "Hey," I said. "Could you give me a French braid when we get to class?" I hated the way it dried after swim class, in dull matted clumps.

Autumn's shoulder-length hair was twisted into two perfectly symmetrical blond sections. She could make it that good without a mirror. "Here," she said, pulling off my tortoiseshell headband before dropping a step behind me. "I'll do it now."

That's how we walked through the freshman hallway, me leading Autumn by my hair, like we were elephants. I kept my head down and asked her questions from my Western Philosophy notes while she went to work, my scalp tightening with every weave. Our first quiz was in five minutes. We'd studied on the phone together the night before, so it was really more of a review, but Autumn had still gotten a few easy ones wrong.

"I can't believe it." Autumn stopped walking, only I didn't realize it until my head snapped back. She sighed and asked, "Were we ever that young?"

I could tell that Autumn was trying to soak up all the excitement and possibility exuding from the freshmen mulling around us. She was completely charmed by their goofiness, bad skin, and awkward roughhousing. She smiled so wide, the skin around her blue eyes wrinkled.

I smiled, too. Except I wasn't thinking back so much as trying to hold on to every minute of senior year. If our dream colleges accepted us, Autumn and I would be living on opposite sides of the country in eleven months. The realist in me had to accept that things wouldn't be the same . . . or at least, not nearly as good as how we had it right now. Autumn would make new friends. Hopefully, I would, too. But it wasn't a prospect I was particularly excited about.

"Oh, jeez," she whispered. "Natalie! Look!"

Autumn nudged her chin toward a curvy girl with black corkscrew curls. The girl was kneeling on the floor, reaching deep into a messy locker for her books. Her pleated uniform skirt tipped forward like a ringing church bell. A small triangle of lavender mesh barely shielded her rear from the entire hallway.

Though it wasn't actually written anywhere in the *Ross Academy Handbook*, it still seemed like every girl at school knew enough to wear something *un*revealing underneath her uniform skirt. Spandex shorts, boxers, leggings, or at the very least, a pair of hipster underwear. Every girl but this poor, clueless freshman.

I debated whether or not to say something. But only for a second, because if I had a piece of spinach in my teeth, or if my zipper was down, I'd rather be told than make a complete fool of myself. Embarrassing moments had a surprisingly long shelf life at our school. One minute you were a normal girl, and the next, you'd be known as Ass Flasher for the next four years. It seemed only right to intervene.

I handed my notebook to Autumn. "Reread my notes on the Socratic method. I'll be right back." I bounded across the hallway, my braid unraveling with every step.

A couple of freshman boys had taken notice of the free show and were panting at this girl's butt. I stared them down and positioned myself to block their view.

"Hey," I said to the girl. "Can I talk to you for a second?"

She stared up at me from the floor, her tan face appearing slightly lighter around her eyes, probably from lying out with an oversize pair of sunglasses. "Um. Sure." Her voice was both friendly and suspicious.

"I'm Natalie Sterling," I said, feeling like I probably should introduce myself. "What's your name?"

She blinked a few times and then stood up. Which, to my great relief, solved the immediate problem of her unfortunate underwear choice. "Hold on — you're *Natalie Sterling*?"

"Um. Yes," I said. And suddenly I turned into the suspicious one.

Her brown eyes were big and expectant, glittering like the eye shadow dusting her lids. She waited, and not exactly patiently, for me to recognize her. "You don't know who I am, do you?" She didn't sound angry. If anything, she seemed tickled.

My mind cycled through the faces at my SAT summer prep course. But this girl was clearly a freshman, so that didn't make sense. I shrugged apologetically. "Are you sure you don't have me confused with someone else?"

"Okay." She closed her eyes and shook her head back and forth a few times, really fast. "I can't believe I'm about to do this." And then, after a deep breath, she danced a jig, right there in front of her locker.

Her toned legs kicked and sliced the air like scissors, and her flats hit the linoleum floor in loud slaps that made everyone take notice. My own deficiency in dance kept me from knowing if she was good or just trying hard. Either way, she bounced with such fervor that her curls boinged like a thousand tiny springs. After a final twirl, which honestly couldn't have come quickly enough, she threw out her hands and exclaimed "River Dance!" Except she said it with a terrible Irish brogue, and it sounded more like *Reevah Daaaanse!*

That's when it hit me.

"Spencer Biddle?" The eight-year-old girl I'd babysat for an entire summer when I turned twelve? Spencer Biddle, who wouldn't use the upstairs bathroom without someone standing outside the door, who would eat macaroni and cheese only if the cheese were orange, who put on elaborate Irish step-dancing shows in her living room?

Her chest heaved as she caught her breath. "I'm honestly relieved you *didn't* recognize me. It's been like . . . what? Almost six years? I'd better look completely different."

"Don't worry," I said, squinting past her makeup and imagining her shiny curls uncoiling to a frizzy and unkempt little girl fro. "You definitely do."

Spencer pushed some wet hair off my shoulder. "I hardly recognized you, either. I mean, look at how grown up and beautiful you are!" It was a weird compliment, like something my Aunt Doreen or Grammy would say. Not someone three years younger than me. "Seriously, Natalie?" she continued. "You were the nicest babysitter I ever had. I remember one time when you threatened to make Eddie Guavera eat rocks when he peed on the flowers we'd just planted around the mailbox."

I winced. "Did I really?"

Spencer laughed the same way she used to — quiet puffs of air that pulsed out of her nose, rapid-fire. "All the neighbor boys were afraid of you. It was so awesome!"

"Didn't your family move to St. Louis?"

"Yeah. When my mom got remarried. But she divorced my stepdad, so we came back this summer." I nodded, even though it felt weird to be discussing things like divorce with Spencer. I was pretty sure that our last conversation involved me trying to convince her that Lucky Charms would make a terrible pizza topping. "We're renting an apartment across Liberty River. It's not bad, actually. My room has these big mirrored closet doors where I can practice my routines."

"You'd dance to anything," I recalled. "Commercials. Those wind chimes your mom hung on the front porch. The sound of the phone ringing." I had a sudden memory of how annoying that actually was, from a babysitter's perspective. I could hardly get Spencer to sit still.

Spencer's glossy smile gave way to a pucker. "Wait. If you didn't recognize me, why did you come over here in the first place?"

I picked some lint off my skirt and suddenly wished that I didn't know the color of Spencer's underwear. I leaned in close enough to smell her cotton-candy perfume and whispered, "When you bent over before, you could see *everything*. And a bunch of boys were enjoying the view."

Her mouth dropped open so wide I could see all her fillings. "Are you kidding?"

I shook my head. Despite being embarrassed, Spencer managed to smile. "You know," I told her, "Ross does offer a pair of uniform pants for the girls, but they're these horrible pleated slacks the color of cardboard. Really, the best thing to do is to wear something underneath your skirt." I gave her the rundown of options, and even lifted my skirt the tiniest bit to show her the navy spandex shorts I always, always wore. Even over tights during winter.

Spencer nodded, but now she was looking behind me, trying to figure out which of the boys had been staring at her.

The warning bell rang. I needed to hurry to class, so I could get settled and focused before the quiz. "I'm sure

I'll see you around, Spencer. And let me know if you have any questions about school stuff."

"Believe me, I definitely plan on exploiting that I'm friends with a senior! All the other freshman girls are going to *die* of jealousy."

I knew that wouldn't actually be true, but hearing Spencer say it made me feel pretty good as I hustled across the hallway to avoid being trampled by our entire football team. Connor Hughes, all tall and lean with his wavy brown hair grazing the collar of his white button-up, led the charge of boys down the hall. He held a playbook in his hands and the rest of his teammates orbited him, peering inside.

Autumn closed my notebook and handed it back to me. "I don't know where you get your courage, Natalie. I couldn't say anything like that to a stranger."

I lifted my eyebrows. "That was no stranger."

I told Autumn the story, and she glanced across the hallway. "So wait. Were you too busy catching up with Spencer that you forgot to tell her about her underwear?"

I turned and saw Spencer bent over again, her butt back on display for everyone.

The eyes of the passing football players flitted to the left, as if Spencer's ass gave off a high-pitched noise at a frequency that only boys could detect. One of the guys, Mike Domski, snatched the binder out from Connor's hands and flapped it furiously toward Spencer's rear end, trying to make a strong enough breeze so her skirt would flutter up even higher. The rest of the team fell all over each other in a fit of laughter.

A sour feeling rippled across my stomach.

Spencer spun around and pressed up against her locker, a look of pretend embarrassment, feigned modesty, painted on her face. The same one I'd fallen for a moment ago.

"Looks like Spencer's grown up to be quite a lady," Autumn said.

She meant it as a joke, I think. Except neither of us laughed.

CHAPTER TWO

I left extra, extra early the next morning, and picked up two egg sandwiches and two Oranginas from the bagel shop on Main Street. It was the first official day of student council elections, and I wanted to get my posters hung up before anyone else, claim the best wall real estate. When I got to Autumn's house, I beeped my car horn along with the song snippet played in between NPR news stories. Across the street, an old lady in a flowered nightgown stared me down from behind her screen door. I mouthed an embarrassed apology.

Autumn finally appeared, darting across her lawn in bare feet. Her black flats were perched on top of the books clutched in her hands, a pair of wrinkled cream-colored knee socks slung over her shoulder. My campaign posters were tucked under her arm.

"Careful you don't bend them!" I called.

I could tell Autumn hadn't bothered to shower that morning, preferring instead to sleep an extra twenty minutes. I had always been an early riser, but Autumn loved to sleep, so I'd make sure to always have a book underneath my pillow whenever we had sleepovers. Lately, I only read SAT prep guides, but that's how I devoured the entire Goosebumps series during middle school — next to my snoring best friend.

Autumn crouched down to the open passenger window and tipped her books forward, causing her shoes to fall onto the seat. She brightened when she saw the white paper bag. "Ooh! Breakfast!"

"Your reward for getting up early to help me."

"I don't need a reward," she said, throwing her books in the backseat and then gently laying my posters on top. "After all, I'm your unofficial campaign manager."

"I wish you'd be my *official* vice president," I said under my breath.

Autumn sighed as she dropped into the passenger seat and clicked her seat belt into the latch with way more force than necessary. "Natalie. You have to let this go."

I'd posed the idea countless times during the summer and as recently as this weekend, when we'd stayed up until three in the morning painting campaign posters. I'd painted one poster with both of our names on it, but Autumn just complained that I'd wasted a perfectly good piece of oak tag. "Good ideas are hard to let go," I said.

She took a big bite of sandwich and got some ketchup on her face. I handed her a napkin. "Look," she said, in between chews. "It means a lot to me that you think I could actually do something like this. But it's not like I need to be vice president to help with all your projects. I'll still be at every student council meeting, just like I've been the last three years."

"It's not about you showing up to meetings. It's about you living up to your full potential, Autumn. You always say that you're more of a *behind-the-scenes* person. But that's not true. It's just a convenient excuse not to be noticed. College admissions counselors don't just want to know that you've participated in extracurricular activities. They want to see leadership skills. That you can take charge of something."

Autumn opened her Orangina and chugged down about five huge gulps. A tiny part of me thought she might be considering it. Then she changed the subject, asking, "What were some of those funny slogans we came up with? I was trying to remember them this morning."

I couldn't force my best friend to run for student council. I knew she had to want it for herself. But that didn't make it any less frustrating.

For the rest of the ride to school, we tried to remember the corny slogans that made us laugh so hard this weekend. Like *Vote For Natalie — She'll Do Things Nattily!* Except without being sugar-drunk on Dr Pepper and cookie dough, they weren't really funny at all.

Ours was the first car in the student parking lot. Ross Academy looked beautiful, the sun rising behind the fieldstone walls, sparking off the dew on the thick lawn. I was so taken with the beauty of our school that it wasn't until I'd gotten halfway up the path when I noticed that every single window had been covered over with white paper.

"That's weird," I said.

"Looks like Kevin Stroop's seriously stepping up his game," Autumn said.

"I guess." Kevin Stroop was last year's treasurer and, as far as I knew, the only person running against me for president. I'd been counting on an easy campaign, mainly because I was last year's vice president, but also because Kevin had made a stupid accounting error that had nearly left us bankrupt. We'd had to enforce a strict one-slice-per-person rule at the end-of-the-year pizza party, which no one had been happy about.

I pulled open the main door and hundreds of pieces of paper fluttered with the fall breeze I'd invited in. They weren't just taped to the windows. Our entire school had been wallpapered — the bathroom doors, bulletin boards, every locker, and the trophy case. An empty plastic tape dispenser crunched beneath my loafer as I stepped forward. Several dozen others were discarded on the floor, down the length of the hallway.

I knew Kevin didn't have the chops to pull off a stunt this big.

I pulled a single sheet from the spout of a water fountain.

It was a piece of photocopied notebook paper, with a bunch of flaming footballs drawn on it, and a cartoon version of Mike Domski, smoking a cigar and flanked by two busty bikini girls.

Unfortunately, this drawing was no sick fantasy. Mike Domski actually got girls to like him. Sure, he was a football player, and, yeah, he hung out with the popular kids. But the guy was a total scumbag, preying on girls too stupid to know better. There seemed to be a sad learning curve on that sort of thing.

Underneath his drawing, he'd actually written *Domski 4 Prez*. And he hadn't even bothered to rip the page out properly — the bottom left corner was missing and he had proudly photocopied the jagged paper fringe.

"Mike Domski," I said aloud.

"You're kidding." Autumn grabbed the flyer and made a face. "Ew. Why's Mike Domski running for student council?"

I actually had to think about it. "Maybe to help his college applications? Or just to be an ass." That was really all the reason someone like Mike would need.

"I'm going to take so much satisfaction in watching you annihilate him." Autumn searched a nearby wall. "What are we going to do with all your posters? He's left no room to hang them up. This can't be legal! Do you want me to try and find Ms. Bee?"

"Don't worry," I said. And then I taped my biggest poster right over a bunch of Mike Domski's stupid cartoon grins.

By lunch, Mike's posters had begun to disappear. I wondered if Ms. Bee had gotten word that he'd charmed the school secretary for use of her copier and deemed them against election rules. But no. Kids had been ripping them down on purpose. I watched a line of guys in the cafeteria ask Mike to autograph them, because they'd be "worth something" someday. Which basically made me want to puke.

Over the rest of the week, I did my best to ignore Mike Domski. It wasn't hard. He wasn't in any AP classes, and we certainly didn't have any friends in common. Still, even from afar, watching him ham up his whole candidacy drove me crazy. The way he'd strut around making ridiculous decrees in old English that started with *henceforth* and ended with *evermore*, and demanded that people address him as *Prez*.

But I stayed calm and collected, even when Mike took direct aim at me. It really didn't bother me all that much. Probably because I was one of a rare few at Ross Academy to see guys like Mike for who they really were — power-drunk meatheads who'd do anything to get a laugh. High school was the best Mike Domski's life would ever get. You could see his entire depressing future written on his dopey face. He'd get into some mediocre college, fall in love with a pregnant stripper, lose all his money to a get-rich-quick internet scheme. I might have even felt bad for Mike Domski, if he hadn't been acting like such a jerk.

But Autumn hated watching Mike make fun of me, and no matter how stupid his insults were, it ate away at her. Like this one time in the cafeteria, when Mike stood underneath one of the banners we'd painted together, flashing two thumbs-up and screaming something about me having *wicked bubble letter skills*.

Autumn's cheeks blushed the most awful shade of purpley red, the same as the undercooked steak on her tray. She kept her eyes locked on that steak, pushing a gristly piece back and forth with a plastic fork that was about to snap in her death grip. And then, without warning, she shot straight up, bumping our table so hard my soda splashed on my lab worksheet.

"Leave her alone," she said, overenunciating each word in as stern a voice as someone as sweet as Autumn could muster. I looked up at her with a half-smile, shocked that she'd had the guts to say anything. She was shaking, the tiniest quivers. My heart broke, knowing what a good friend I had in Autumn. If that was hard for anyone to do, it was hardest for her.

Mike reacted like Autumn had suddenly appeared out of thin air, with phony surprise and awe. He strutted over to our table, sniffing the air like a bloodhound tracking a scent, and stopped right in front of her. "Hey, Fish Sticks! I didn't smell you there!"

Those words sucked the air out of the entire cafeteria. I couldn't move. I couldn't look at Autumn. I just listened through the silence for her next to me, praying that she remembered to breathe.

I had always wondered when the rest of the school would figure out that joke wasn't funny anymore. Or maybe it was something closer to hope. Hope that, with each passing year, people would forget. But in that moment, I finally understood that would never happen. Someone would say it at our twentieth reunion, and Autumn would have to explain it to her husband. *Fish Sticks* would get a cheap laugh, somewhere, for the rest of our lives. It was too easy. Too mean. And I found it piercingly unfair that someone like Mike Domski would never comprehend how much those two words destroyed my beautiful best friend.

Anger rose up inside me like lava. I reached for the closest object and hurled it at Mike. That turned out to be my slice of pizza, and it hit him square in the chest, leaving a triangle stain of oil and sauce and hot pepper flakes behind on his shirt before it fell with a splat on his brown suede shoes.

"Oops," I said in my most unsorry voice. A bunch of people gasped, and I even got a few laughs.

Mike curled his lip. "Damn. You know what? I threw out the student council handbook Ms. Bee gave me. But I'm sure I saw a whole section about election rules and the kinds of stunts that could disqualify a candidate. Tell you what, Natalie — I'll double-check if she has an extra copy and let you know."

I rolled my eyes as Mike stalked off. But really, inside, I panicked. Had I ruined everything, just to defend Autumn's honor? Had I handed the entire election over, the thing I'd been dreaming about and working toward for the last three years, to Mike Domski?

Tears welled up in Autumn's eyes. "Come on," I said, stuffing our things into my book bag. I didn't want her to humiliate herself even more. "Let's go to the library."

"I'm so sorry, Natalie," she whispered. "I hope I didn't get you in trouble. I'll die if you get disqualified!"

Autumn moved too slow, so I grabbed her hand and pulled her along. "You didn't have to defend me like that," I muttered. If she could have just ignored Mike like I did, this wouldn't have happened.

She shook her head. "That's what best friends do for each other," she said with resolve. Autumn wiped her eyes with one hand, and with the other, she squeezed mine tight, the way I'd always squeezed hers.

CHAPTER THREE

I am not an *every cloud has a silver lining* type of person, but one undeniably good thing did come out of the original Fish Sticks debacle: It saved my friendship with Autumn.

Autumn and I had met forever ago at the pool. We were six, and our moms had signed us both up for swimming lessons. Autumn had gone to Ross Academy since kindergarten, but I went to public school, so I'd never seen her before.

I noticed her right away. Her blond hair was light like the underside of a lemon peel, and it hung all the way to her waist. I liked the way it floated through the water, and watched with utter fascination as it turned green from the chlorine over the course of our lessons.

But that's not why I really noticed her. It was because Autumn was the most spastic swimmer in the pool. She'd splash more than anyone else and always looked somewhat distressed.

When the lifeguard made us partners, I groaned, because each lesson ended with a kickboard race and the winners got to pick a Jolly Rancher out of a big glass bowl in the pool office. I pretty much knew Autumn and I would never have a chance. We didn't, either. We never won a single Jolly Rancher. Even though I was probably the fastest kickboarder in the pool, I could never go fast enough to compensate for her.

I would've been mad . . . but Autumn was so nice. Once, I'd shared my towel when she'd forgotten hers, and she said *thank you* about a million times. And she was surprisingly silly, too. She taught me how to make a particular kind of fist, that when you squeezed, it would shoot a stream of water.

Except those things didn't exactly make us friends, just girls who swam together. My parents both had extremely demanding jobs — Mom at her architecture firm, and Dad at his ophthalmology practice. Either one would show up at exactly five minutes to three, and I'd get put in the car, even before I'd had a chance to properly dry off. Autumn, on the other hand, would make plans to play with one girl or another as soon as she was out of the pool, like swim class was a warm-up for the fun she was about to have.

It wasn't until the very last lesson, when the lifeguard

let kids jump off the highest diving platform, that Autumn and I bonded for real.

Autumn froze with terror, but I forced her up the ladder with me. Mainly because none of the other girls in class would do it, probably because they all wore two-pieces and a jump that big could easily make you lose your top. They hung near the shallow end and laughed as the boys leaped off and did ninja kicks or screamed like Tarzan. I wasn't scared, but it did feel like we were climbing forever. At the top, I laced our wrinkly fingers together and counted to three before jumping. Well, I jumped. Autumn sort of got pulled along with me, screaming the whole way down and getting water up her nose once we plunged in.

She doggy-paddled out of the pool, coughing hard. I followed her, feeling terrible, and decided that I would sit out with her for the rest of the lesson. Instead, Autumn raced to the ladder. She kept jumping. On her own. Each time, she'd spring a little higher, a bit farther out. I loved watching her test herself. Autumn had real courage, buried deep down inside her. All she'd needed was a push from me.

We announced ourselves as best friends when our moms arrived to pick us up that day.

Autumn and I were definitely an odd couple. She would show up at my house in a skirt and sandals, even though I'd tell her I wanted to try to get the boys down the block to invite us to play Manhunt. She'd say I was the worst fingernail painter in history, and that she'd do a better job with her left hand than I'd do with my right.

I wasn't a tomboy. Sure, I'd wear my cousin Noah's hand-me-downs, but sometimes I'd pick out a sundress, even if we weren't going to church or out to dinner. I had a collection of stuffed bears that lived in a nylon hammock strung over my bed and I cried like a baby the time Christopher Clark threw a garden snake he'd found behind his garage at me. But before Autumn, I really never had any friends who were girls. None lived on my street.

Autumn was like fizzy water, light and bubbly. I always knew it, but when I transferred to Ross Academy for junior high, it really became clear. For the first time, I saw how effortlessly Autumn made friends, much more easily than I did. So many people would say hi to her in the halls. I remember feeling lucky that I had gotten in early. Lucky, and a little nervous.

She'd get invited to sleepovers. She'd have girls wanting to sit next to her at lunch. Even though Autumn stuck by me, I could still feel her drifting away. Not intentionally, of course. But I think saying *no* to invitations and trying to score me pity invites had started to get a little old for both of us.

Autumn explained I could be a know-it-all sometimes, only she said it in a much more polite and gentle way. I didn't deny it. My parents were both intellectual types, and that sort of thing permeated everything we did as a family. We had our kitchen radio always tuned in to NPR. We did brainteasers over dinner. We shared the Sunday paper. And family vacations were to science centers or fossil expeditions or historical monuments. Maybe it made me weird, but it definitely made me smarter than most people I knew. But smart didn't necessarily cut it in junior high.

I had invited Autumn to come with my family to a laser show at the planetarium. Her face fell, and she explained that she'd accepted an invitation from Marci Cooperstein's family to visit their lake house for a week.

I played it cool, but inside I steamed. Marci had been trying to edge in on my friendship with Autumn for months. Autumn had held Marci off, but I guess the promise of Jet Skis and barbeques and bunk beds were too much for her to resist. It was seven days of pure misery for me. I made my mom take me to the library about four different times, because all I did was sit in my room and read. By that time, the other kids on the block weren't friends, only boys to feel awkward around. I had no one else.

When Autumn did come back, tanner than I'd ever seen her, she slept over four nights straight and gave me a friendship bracelet she'd made especially for me, courtesy of Marci's bead kit. She had used the nicest beads, too — lavender glass spheres alternating with iridescent stones shaped like tiny grains of rice. Every time Marci saw that bracelet, she seethed. I wore it until the string broke, and then I picked up all the beads I could find. I still have a few in my jewelry box.

I guess that kind of competition should have prepared me for Chad, but it didn't. Guys were not a part of our equation. We didn't even talk about them. That probably sounds weird, but our friendship had this strange, timeless innocence about it. And though I knew I could compete with the Marci Coopersteins of the world, I was no match for Chad. Chad swept Autumn completely off her feet.

Once I was at her house practicing a dialogue for our French project when Chad called and invited Autumn to meet him and some friends down near Liberty River. Autumn assumed I wouldn't want to go, but I told her I would. It made me happy, how excited she was to have me go with her. Excited, until she gently urged me to change into one of her sweaters and to try some of her berry lip gloss.

I had a weird feeling when Autumn took my hand and we veered off the sidewalk into a thin patch of woods. We followed a worn stretch of dirt, littered with trash and a few cigarette butts. I was pretty disoriented even though I could hear the river, but Autumn walked like she was both Lewis *and* Clark. After a few twists and turns, we came upon a big boulder, perched over the silvery water. A bunch of guys sat on it, drinking beers and blowing smoke into the night sky. We were the only girls there.

Looking back, I definitely overreacted. But older boys and beers and dark, dark woods were so far out of my realm of experience. After about ten minutes, I pretended to feel sick. Autumn knew I was faking, and let me walk home by myself.

She only invited Marci Cooperstein after that.

I thought I'd lost her.

Then the Fish Sticks incident happened, and I was the one person who stood by her. To everyone else at school, she was tainted. The boys were grossed out by her, and even some girls were snooty and snotty and suddenly too good for her. Marci actually laughed a few times at the jokes other people made. Right in front of Autumn.

I told Marci that she was pathetic.

And then I happily picked up the slack. I walked in front of Autumn, or struck up a loud conversation about absolutely nothing, casting the best friend force field to distract her from the sniffers and the stinky faces. I think some people were afraid of me. I became known as the nerdy girl with the scary intensity who'd do anything to protect Fish Sticks.

A couple of weeks later, Marci apologized to Autumn in a note she'd written during chorus. Autumn showed it to me. It was full of grammatical errors. *Your right to be mad at me*, Marci wrote. Idiot.

I thought Autumn would write Marci back, but she crumpled up the note and flushed it down the toilet. I'd never been more proud of her.

With my help, Autumn turned her negative into a positive. Together we channeled our energy into school-work. Autumn was never a great student, and that first semester of freshman year, she'd nearly failed out from the stress of everything that had happened. But I helped her come around. We'd take our lunch in the library and study or do homework together. I even got her involved with student council. Autumn still didn't do well enough to make it into AP classes, but she made regular honor roll, and so long as she didn't royally screw up her SATs, she'd have her pick of colleges.

After Chad Rivington, Autumn never had another boyfriend. It saved her from a lot of needless heartbreak. And me, well, the whole thing just let me be a good best friend. Which was all I'd wanted to do in the first place.

CHAPTER FOUR

On Monday, I found one of my posters taped to the wall above my locker. The Friday before, it had hung near the main office, and my original pieces of masking tape were still stuck to the corners. The poster had a picture of me on it, holding a jacket in each hand during last year's winter coat drive. It read, *Vote for Natalie, A Leader with Experience.*

Mike (obviously) had taken a marker and done some doodling at my expense. He had given me a moustache, drawn two enormous penises (one for each of my hands) and a bunch of question marks hovering over my head. He'd crossed out *leader* and written *VIRGIN* on top of it. And squeezed the word *NO* in before *experience*.

The hallway was empty, but it wouldn't be for long. The classrooms were still locked from the weekend, so I couldn't grab a chair. After jumping up a few times in a desperate and unsuccessful attempt to reach the poster, I headed straight for Ms. Bee's office, walking so fast that my kneesocks slid down my calves.

I had expected Mike Domski to retaliate for Friday's pizza incident, of course. I knew he'd want to embarrass me like I'd embarrassed him. But his attack was worse than any grease stain. It was degrading.

Ms. Bee sat at her desk, blowing through the cloud blossoming from the ceramic cup cradled in her hands. Even though she was in her early sixties, Ms. Bee was tan and fit and beautiful, in a loose black linen dress, a tangle of turquoise and red glass beads, and leather slides the color of honey. Her thick white hair curled off her forehead like the crest of an ocean wave and pooled at her shoulders. She had a stack of papers and folders before her. It took a few seconds, and a small fake cough, for her to notice me lingering outside.

Ms. Bee looked up and said, "Natalie. Good. I wanted to talk with you today. Come in. And close the door behind you."

I was too angry to sit, so I stood just inside her office with the doorknob pressing into my back. "Mike Domski defaced one of my posters." My voice quivered, and I sounded like a little baby. I hated that Mike could get under my skin so bad.

"Are you sure it was him?"

"Yes." I glanced at the clock above her head. If we

didn't act fast, students would soon be arriving, looking at that poster, laughing at me.

"You saw him do it?"

"No." My face burned. "But I know it was Mike. And he wrote terrible things about me." I thought about telling her exactly what terrible things, only I was too mortified.

"I see." Ms. Bee set her cup down. "Is it true you threw a slice of pizza at Mr. Domski last Friday?"

My chin hit my chest. "Yes, I did."

Each semester, I'd drive my guidance counselor crazy, shifting requirements around so I could take every single history class Ms. Bee taught, even her electives like Vietnam and the '60s, which were way harder than electives like ceramics, but incredibly interesting. She supplemented her lectures with personal photos, memorabilia, even reading from her own diary. I had always wanted to impress her. And now, thanks to Mike Domski, I'd done the opposite.

She took off her glasses, an angular pair of black frames, and slid them into a silk pouch. "Despite the fact that you're upset, I must admit that I'm glad to hear about this poster issue. I was worried that I might have to discipline you, but since Mr. Domski has also chosen to take a less-than-dignified route in this campaign, these infractions can cancel each other out." She leaned back until her wooden chair creaked. "Can I give you a little friendly advice, one girl to another?" I nodded. "Boys like Mr. Domski are intimidated by powerful women, Natalie. The only way he can think to belittle you is for simply being a female. But you must remain as strong and poised as you have been the last three years of high school. You must not let him beat you in this election."

A burst of energy flew through me. Ms. Bee was right. Mike could only resort to low blows because I out-matched him in every legitimate way.

Ms. Bee pulled open a desk drawer and rooted around. "I wish I could say that you won't meet a million more Mike Domskis in the course of your lifetime, but I'm afraid that simply isn't true." She handed me a glossy pamphlet. "There's a leadership conference for young women in Boston during our spring break. It's going to address exactly these sorts of challenges. The woman who runs it was my roommate during my master's program, and I might be able to work out some kind of discount for you. Or at least the opportunity to network directly with some incredibly inspiring women at the very top of their fields. If you haven't already packed your bikinis for Cancun" — she grinned — "I think it could be a formative experience for you."

"Thank you," I said. But really, those two words didn't even come close.

I walked back to my locker with my head held high. The hallway was starting to get thick with students, the height of the morning rush. I found an empty trash can I could flip over and climb on, to be tall enough to rip the poster down. But I didn't need to. Someone had beaten me to it.

CHAPTER FIVE

On election day, I sat between Mike and Kevin in the front of the library. Kevin was a couple of inches away, but Mike was so painfully close that the arms of our chairs were touching.

His left leg bounced up and down in a khaki blur, and the floorboards creaked sharp sounds that stabbed straight into my forehead. He did it on purpose, of course. Anything to rattle me. My pleated skirt crinkled up underneath my thighs, itching me like crazy, but I wouldn't move. Not an inch. I didn't want to risk touching Mike by accident. I didn't even want our uniforms to touch.

What seemed like the entire school had gathered to hear the results. Connor Hughes sat in the front row, his tie loose around his neck, turning when someone behind him started chanting, *"Dom-ski Dom-ski Dom-ski."* A bunch of other voices joined in the chorus. The whole room got loud, and I suddenly had trouble swallowing the syrupy dissolve from my peppermint Life Saver.

In a perfect world, this would be no contest. The most qualified candidate would win. But Mike Domski had a lot more friends than I did. A lot more.

I quickly tried to prepare myself, in case things didn't go my way. I envisioned myself having to smile, to shake Mike's hand, because that's what a gracious loser does. I wiped my palms against my bare legs. They felt clammy. Cold.

As tough as that would be, I refused to give Mike the satisfaction of humiliating me on top of everything else. I forbade myself to cry if I lost. I'd drown my insides before I let a single tear roll down my cheek. That's exactly what he'd want. Natalie Sterling, crying over a student council election.

Losing wouldn't even be the worst part. The worst part would be quitting student council. I didn't want to, of course, but what else could I do? I decided it was best to write a resignation letter to Ms. Bee instead of telling her in person, so she wouldn't try to convince me to stick it out. I couldn't do that to myself. And as much as I knew Ms. Bee would be disappointed, she wouldn't want my participation to come at the price of my dignity. I knew what would happen — Mike would get bored with all the responsibility and work, and push everything on my lap. He'd try to make me into his personal secretary, someone he could boss around. And there was absolutely no way I could deal with that.

Ms. Bee sat inside the library office. I watched her through the glass, her head down as she counted ballots. Her forehead seemed more wrinkled than usual, which worried me for obvious reasons. I sat up tall and tried to make eye contact.

"Nervous?"

Mike smugly stared me down, thick-as-caterpillar eyebrows touching over his nose. I pressed my lips together tight and ignored him. A smirk spread across his face, and he rubbed the dusty black of his stubbly chin. Of course Mike didn't bother to shave for election day. "I have to say, Natalie, your level of intensity is pretty hot." He gently patted his lap. "I'm actually getting a chubby."

I glanced over at Kevin Stroop, his eyes burning holes through the floor. It could have been a campaign strategy. Let Mike and me duke it out, while Kevin cleaned house. Though I doubted it. More likely, Kevin feared Mike Domski, or he just didn't care if a guy said such disgusting things to a girl.

Not that I needed Kevin to stand up for me. I could

handle this myself. "Stop talking to me," I declared, which fell far short of the sharp retort I'd hoped to conjure up.

"Hey! Come on, Natalie. I'm only kidding with you." His smile lengthened to a sneer. "You could *never* give me a hard-on. You're like . . . dick repellant."

Anger burned hot through my body, and I gripped the sides of my chair. Mike Domski wanted to hurt me, and the best way he knew was to call me ugly. I hated that, despite the fact that I would rather eat vomit than touch a hair on Mike's head, it worked. It took all my self-control not to hock the biggest, wettest ball of spit right between Mike's eyes. And I would have, too, if not for Ms. Bee weaving through the thick crowd, waving a slip of paper over her head. "Okay! Thank you for your patience! Here we go!"

Spencer lurked near the doorway, huddled with a couple of other girls. When our eyes met, she gave a big wave and blew me a kiss, which was a gesture more baffling than comforting. I tried to find Autumn's face in the crowd, but when I couldn't, I settled on the wall to my left, where the senior portraits of former Ross Academy student council presidents hung. Most were boys in blazers, wearing grins dripping with unabashed, unapologetic ambition. There were only a handful of girls, all stern-faced with set jaws. I felt the kinship straight away.

Ms. Bee joined us in the front of the library. The smell of her peppery perfume comforted me, just a little. "It's wonderful to see so many of you interested in student council this year," she said. "Our first meeting will be on Monday, and I hope you'll parlay this enthusiasm and sign up for one of our many committees."

I waited, a hollow smile frozen on my face, and listened to the names of the winners. David Goss won secretary. Dipak Shah won treasurer. Martin Gedge took vice president. I smiled at Martin to congratulate him, and he gave a worried look that cut right through me.

The stuffy library air fluttered with the tepid applause of people waiting for the main event. Ms. Bee cleared her throat and the room went quiet. All except for my heart, which pounded rapid and crazy.

"And in the election for your new student council president, we may have had our closest results in my history as an adviser. The winner, by just a handful of votes, is . . . Na —"

Somebody in Mike's crowd booed, and I never heard the rest of my name. Not that it mattered.

From somewhere in the back of the room, Autumn

barreled through the crowd toward me, knocking people aside with her huge book bag. Her hair flopped all in her face, and she screamed at the top of her lungs. I rose to my feet, smiling so hard it hurt. Autumn wrapped her arms around me tight, and we swayed with such force that we almost fell on the floor. We jumped up and down, over and over, both of us screaming and laughing.

I noticed Mike standing with his friends. Connor grinned at me. He thought my celebration was funny, I guess. But Mike could barely conceal his disgust.

I broke free from Autumn and pushed myself in front of him. I knew I had huge damp spots in the armpits of my white shirt, but I didn't care. After pulling up my hair into a quick ponytail, I stuck out my hand and waited for Mike to shake it. "Don't you want to congratulate me?" I said in my most sarcastic voice. His friends were all listening. Connor Hughes. Everyone. And I loved every second of it.

Mike looked down at my hand and scoffed. "Congratulations on being the kind of loser this stuff actually matters to."

Before I could say anything back, Autumn pulled me away. "You okay, Miss President?" she asked, and massaged my shoulders like a boxer and his trainer after a long fight. The library had begun to empty out, but there were still lots of students who stuck around to congratulate me. The moment felt so right, so beautiful. Like destiny. Like all those life-changing moments should feel. Easy.

CHAPTER SIX

I picked up Autumn later that night. It was supposed to be, at least to her knowledge, our typical Friday — renting whatever movie was next on our list (we'd been working our way through the AFI Top 100 Films list, which I'd cut from the newspaper and dutifully laminated at my mom's office), followed by snacks, followed by either face masks or new nail polish, followed by whatever lame show was on television until we fell asleep.

Except I had heard on NPR during breakfast that *A Streetcar Named Desire* was playing at a little independent movie theater a few towns over. It wasn't actually the next film on our list, but the chance to see one on the big screen was too exciting to pass up. Plus, it would make for a more special night, considering I'd won the election a few hours before.

Even though my air-conditioning was on, everything still felt sticky. September weather always left you guessing, with some days hot like summer and others chilly like fall.

I beeped and Autumn came running out in jeans and an oversize hoodie I'd bought her on one of my college tours. I felt a little bad, because I was in a red corduroy skirt, a black scoop neck, and the tiny silver hoops Grammy had given me on my Sweet Sixteen. Not that we needed to dress up, but this particular movie theater was a lot different than the megaplex inside Summit Mall. It served wine and had gourmet snacks, like kettle corn and Italian chocolate bars. A red-velvet curtain hid the screen until just before the film started, and they showed movie trailers in French and Italian.

Autumn knew something was up as soon as she saw me. "What's going on?" she asked, smiling. "Where are we going?"

"It's a secret," I teased.

"But you look so nice. Should I go change?"

I would have said sure, but Autumn was slow enough getting ready for school, never mind when she actually had a choice of outfits. Anyway, she always looked pretty. I shook my head. "Don't worry. You look fine."

I decided to take back roads, to keep Autumn guessing — a wandering maze of rolling hills and twisted streets that made our stomachs drop, so long as I hit the gas at just the right moment. Together we sang whatever song came on, my pathetic radio turned up so loud the speakers crackled. My heart felt buoyant, lifted by my relief over the election and the excitement of surprising Autumn. It seemed less like driving and more like we were floating.

Autumn kept guessing about what I had planned. Then she pointed out the window and looked all excited.

"No way!" she gasped. "We're going to a party?"

Her words didn't make sense to me at first. We weren't anywhere near the theater. I had to come down from the clouds and look around to figure them out.

Cars were crammed along every available inch of curbside, parked in haste, as if the beer supply might run out at any second. I recognized some by their Ross Academy bumper stickers. Music thumped from a small house halfway down the street, bursting with people. Some kids were hanging out on a lawn, blanketed by fall leaves no one had bothered to rake up.

All I could come up with was, "Are you kidding?" What in the world would ever make Autumn think I was bringing her to a party?

"So . . . this isn't what we're doing tonight," she said, the excitement draining from her face.

I shook my head. Even though I didn't want to ruin the surprise, I explained what I had planned for us. I tried to sound excited about all the fancy snacks and the velvet curtain, but Autumn didn't look interested. She kept staring out of the passenger window as we passed by the party house.

Finally she turned to face me. "What if we just walked in?"

"Why would we do that?"

"I don't know. To freak everyone out? Not in a bad way. We'd be like . . . celebrities or special guests or something. Plus, we've never been to a party together before, which seems like something we should probably do before we graduate, right? And besides, you look so pretty tonight."

I couldn't believe what she was saying. If there was anything in the whole world I didn't want to do, it was randomly show up at a high school party that I wasn't invited to, full of people we didn't like. And Autumn was delusional if she thought we'd be welcomed with open arms. Not to mention that I had made other plans for us. Better plans.

But I didn't bother saying as much. Instead I pointed out the window at a boy kneeling on the curb, puking into a bush. "Wow. Looks like we're really missing out on an awesome time."

"We should pull over and make sure he's okay, don't you think?"

I looked at the clock. We still had plenty of time to get to the theater, but I was concerned that if I parked to check on this boy, Autumn would make a run for the house, and then I'd have to go chasing after her. So, after locking the doors, I put the car in park and rolled down my window.

"Hey. Puking boy . . . are you okay?"

The boy didn't say anything, or even look in our direction. Instead, he waved and gave us a thumbs-up.

I turned to Autumn. "Can we go now?"

"I guess," she said, all pouty. She turned off my radio, rolled down her window, and strained to make out the music wafting in the air.

I guess was good enough for me. I wasn't going to wait around and give Autumn a chance to change her mind.

Autumn screamed as I hit the gas.

I pressed the brakes as hard and fast as I could, slamming my car to a sudden stop. My headlights rocked up and down the dark street. Four drunken boys stood frozen at my bumper. Mike Domski, Scott Phillips, Paul Zed, and James Rocker.

"Watch where you're going!" I screamed, my quivering hand hovering over the car horn. The smell of burnt rubber wafted though my vents.

The boys' movements kickstarted with uproarious laughter, as they realized imminent death had, just barely, missed its mark. I tried to inch my car forward, but we were pinned by the human roadblock, forced to witness their drunken celebration. They leaped into each other's burly arms and sang a chorus of *holy shit, dude!* Mike Domski tossed aside a beer can and started humping my hood ornament.

"Get off my car!" I shouted.

"I'm trying!" he moaned. "Oh, God, I'm trying!" After Mike pretended to bring my Honda to orgasm, the laughing boys made their way up the front lawn of the party.

"Looks like Mike's over losing the election," Autumn said, trying to sound lighthearted. Then she added, "Are you sure you don't want to go?"

"Why don't I just drop you off?" It came out bitchy, but I couldn't help it.

"Forget it," Autumn said, though she sounded like she was doing anything but.

A shaggy straggler shuffled a few quiet steps behind the pack. Connor Hughes. He stooped to peer inside my window with this curious look on his face. I could smell the beer all over him, warm and sour. "There's a spot down the street," he offered, pointing off into the blackness. His thumbs were threaded through holes in the cuffs of his thermal.

We locked eyes for the briefest of seconds. His were blue and watery, because he'd been drinking and doing who knows what else.

"Thanks for the tip," I said sarcastically, then pressed my foot down on the gas.

Autumn spun around in her seat. "That could be interpreted as an invitation."

I glanced in my rearview mirror, but couldn't see anything. Only night. My heartbeat started to slow. "We're going to be late for the movie."

Autumn turned back around and huffed. "You know, there's something to be said for spontaneity."

I didn't even bother responding. I just drove as fast as I could away from that house.

CHAPTER SEVEN

The rest of my weekend pretty much sucked. Autumn didn't sleep over on Friday or Saturday, but she came over on Sunday to do a few SAT practice exams together. I could tell she wasn't feeling it. I'd look up and she'd be staring out our kitchen window, even though the timer was ticking away and she was at least five test pages behind me. Obviously, practice exams aren't the most fun thing to do, but the SATs were in just over a month, and I wanted us to be as ready as we could possibly be.

Not that it always worked that way. Because even though I'd practiced my speech countless times, I was way more nervous than I'd thought I'd be for the first student council meeting on Monday. I kept trying to remind myself that the stresses of the election had passed. I'd beaten Mike Domski, and now I could finally get down to business.

Before heading to the meeting, I wanted to freshen

up and collect myself. The perfect place to go was the girls' bathroom near the teachers' lounge. Other girls avoided it for the risks of getting caught talking on their cell phones or smoking a cigarette, but the lack of use meant that it was always clean. The dispensers stayed full of syrupy pink soap, and there was always toilet paper and paper towels to be found. It was my favorite place to pee. It was like an executive girls' bathroom.

But I wasn't alone. I opened the door to find Spencer kneeling on the radiator. Her back was arched, and she stretched her head toward the ceiling, like she was in some strange yoga pose.

I flashed her a quick smile and dropped my book bag in the well of a dry sink.

"Shhhh!"

Spencer took her finger off her lips and pointed above her head at the vents in the ceiling. A layer of fuzzy dust sat on each slit. She whispered, "Mrs. Dockey was just bitching about Principal Hurley not approving her costume budget for the school musical. She actually said that she *'can't put on* The Wizard of Oz *with fucking bedsheets and a burlap sack!'*"

We both tried to hold in our laugher, but it was practically impossible. Mrs. Dockey was about eighty years old and completely soft-spoken. I didn't think it was possible for her to curse like that. Then again, she did take the musical theater productions very seriously.

I rifled through my bag for my hairbrush, forcing it through the knots in my hair. I made sure my headband was perched right at the top of my head. I slicked my lips with my tube of Burt's Bees. I looked as ready as I could be, but inside, my stomach was churning. I'd never had the chance to stand out like this before. To be a leader.

"I took your advice," Spencer said to me. "See?" She jumped off the radiator and lifted up her skirt, flashing a pair of pink satiny petticoat underwear with layers of frills across the butt. "These were actually part of my dance costume for this can-can routine I did in a Moulin Rouge show."

I smiled. Not the toothy kind, but the lips pressed together kind. It was . . . a marginal improvement. But I had to give Spencer credit. If she danced in outfits like that, she probably wouldn't get nervous giving a student council speech.

"So, congratulations on winning the election. A few girls in my homeroom were planning to vote for Mike because he was cute, but I forced them to vote for you."

"Thanks," I said, and tucked my shirt into my skirt.

"I saw what Mike did to your poster." She shook her

head disapprovingly. "Though I guess you can't really blame him."

Had Spencer been the one to take it down? I turned to face her. "What do you mean?"

She scrunched her curls in the mirror. "Sexual tension makes guys act like complete idiots."

I raised an eyebrow. There was certainly tension between me and Mike Domski, but it was hardly sexual. Not even close.

Spencer gave me wink, as if I were acting coy. "Mike totally wants to bone you. It's so obvious."

I shook my head emphatically. "Umm, no, he doesn't. We hate each other."

"Seriously?"

"Seriously."

"Okay, maybe on the surface he hates you," Spencer conceded. "But I bet it goes deeper than that." She tapped a finger on her lips a few times, thinking. "He could never get a girl like you. You are so out of his league, it kills him. And all that frustration bubbles up and makes him act the way he does. Honestly, it's textbook boy."

It was nice to hear Spencer say such complimentary things about me, even though she had no idea what she was talking about. But it was also sort of unnerving, listening to her analyze me and Mike like that. What could she possibly know about sexual tension? She was only fourteen.

I zipped up my bag and hoisted it onto my shoulders. I didn't want to be the last one in the library and appear irresponsible. But Spencer leaned against the sink next to mine, blocking my way to the door. She clearly wanted to talk. And maybe it would be cool to be the girl everyone was waiting for. To make a dramatic entrance. I guessed I could spare a couple more minutes.

"So, Spencer. How are your classes going?" I asked.

"Pretty good. I like everything, except for History of Modern Civilization."

"I took that freshman year. It's not actually that hard, so long as you keep up with the reading."

"It's not so much the work as it is the teacher," Spencer groaned.

"What? Are you kidding? Ms. Bee is awesome. She's the best teacher in our entire school."

Spencer looked doubtful. "She doesn't like me."

"I'm sure she does," I said. But really, there was a part of me that wondered if Spencer might be right. Ms. Bee was a tough teacher, and she was hardest on the girls. I liked that about her, but she definitely wasn't going to pander to Spencer's underwear-flashing antics.

"You just have to show her that you care about learning. If she thinks that you aren't interested, then she won't be interested in you." I was afraid that was Spencer's biggest problem. She was concentrating on the wrong things. "Have you joined any clubs?"

"Not yet. I'm still evaluating my options." It was a weird thing to say, because what did Spencer need to evaluate? If you wanted to join a club, you did. There were no limits on that kind of thing. "I really wish our school had a dance team."

"Well, if you join student council, you could propose that to the school board."

"Really? Students have the power to do that?" she asked, and I nodded. "That's awesome. Maybe I'll come to the first meeting. It's tomorrow, right?"

"It's today. In about five minutes, actually." How did she not know this? Spencer had been in the library on Friday, when Ms. Bee announced the meeting. And there were signs posted all over the hallways. I'd hung them up myself.

She pouted. "Shoot. My mom's supposed to take me to the dance studio on Main to sign up for some classes."

"Don't worry," I told her. "You can still be involved in student council, even if you miss today's meeting." I smiled. "And you know me, so you've got the inside track."

"Ooh! Then you're the perfect person to ask. Is it true that we get to wear normal clothes on pep rally day? I heard someone say that in the hallway."

"Yes, so long as you've got on school colors."

"Cool. A few of my friends and I were thinking about designing our own T-shirts. You know, to show school spirit."

Her enthusiasm was a pleasant surprise. "You should definitely meet up with your class rep. We're going to be deciding them today at the meeting, so I don't know who it is yet, but find me tomorrow and I'll tell you. He or she will be in charge of organizing the hall decorations for the freshman class. I'm sure your help would be appreciated. Pep rallies are sort of a big deal here." I felt for the note cards in my chest pocket. "And I have something pretty exciting planned for this year's festivities. Seriously. It's going to be epic."

"Cool." Spencer bit her lip. "I'm sorry, Natalie. I feel like I'm letting you down or something. I wish I could come today."

I wished she could, too. Not that being involved with dance wasn't a good thing. But I had a feeling that Spencer could benefit from a more traditional school activity. One without sexy costumes. "Well, I'm going to be late. And that wouldn't look good at all."

Spencer let out a deep, happy sigh. "I still can't believe how lucky I am that you were my babysitter, and now I'm like automatically friends with the student council president. Honestly, it doesn't get much better than that."

I felt myself blushing.

"Break a leg, Natalie!" she said, throwing up her hand for a high five.

I couldn't remember the last time I'd had one. When I slapped Spencer's hand, it made the best sound.

CHAPTER EIGHT

Heads turned when I entered the library. I was still a few minutes early, but the room was already full. Several wooden tables had been pushed together to make one huge rectangle. I scanned for a vacant seat, until I remembered that mine was the one at the very front of the room.

"Where've you been?" Autumn asked.

"I was talking to Spencer in the bathroom, trying to get her to join student council. I think it could be really beneficial for her." And then I had a great idea. "You should talk to her, Autumn. Tell her how good this was for you."

Her mouth wrinkled up. "What do you mean?"

I could tell she was getting mad, and I guessed this wasn't the best time to get into a conversation about the Fish Sticks incident. "Never mind," I said.

I thought about asking someone to move, so Autumn could sit near me at the front of the room, but before I could, she took a chair in the last row, near the door.

Which sucked, but was probably for the best. I didn't want to look like I was playing favorites with my best friend. And if she had really wanted to sit up front, she would have run for vice president, like I'd suggested.

Dipak fought with the plastic window shades, pulling until they snapped up, exposing the library to a weak September sunlight. Outside, the tops of the trees — fiery reds and oranges and yellows — blazed through the thick leaded glass. Martin leaned over and whispered, "There are a lot of kids here, don't you think?"

I nodded, and tried not to focus on the tiny flake of dandruff floating in a tuft of Martin's wiry black hair.

Ms. Bee shut the doors and the talking quieted. She nodded at me to begin. I stood up and cupped my note cards in my hand.

"Hello, everyone. Thanks for coming," I said, projecting my voice as best as I could, and then flipped to the next card. I probably should have written more than a sentence on each one, but my handwriting was really bad, and I wanted to make sure I could read it. "I am thrilled to have been voted president of student council at Ross Academy, and I call this, our first meeting, to order." A few people clapped, which felt good.

"It's going to be a very busy and exciting year, with lots of expectations on our shoulders. Everyone who participated in student council last year knows that I have enormous shoes to fill." I went on to proudly list the many accomplishments of Will Branch, our most recent president. In addition to his regular student council duties, Will also established a senior lounge with leather couches, filibustered the banning of *The Chocolate War* by storming a secret school board meeting with a Gandhi-inspired sit-in, and coordinated a student-teacher basketball game to raise money for a freshman with leukemia.

Will had set the bar high, but I was going to aim higher. "Rest assured," I said, "I have innovative ideas of my own. Including —"

Just then, the door slowly creaked open, and Spencer stuck her head inside. She had tried to be quiet, but everyone turned to look. "Sorry!" she said, and excused her way through the room, passing plenty of open spots, until she found a place to squeeze in at the table.

Clearly, it wasn't the best timing. But I couldn't be mad. I was happy that Spencer had shown up after all. Not just shown up, but pushed her way to the front, where the older students sat. The girl was fearless. I smiled and flipped to my next card.

"In addition to this year's pep rally festivities, I've

decided that, as my first act as student council president, we will have our very first bonfire, to take place immediately after the football team annihilates Saint Ann's." Whispers instantly overtook the room. People were excited. It was exactly the reaction I'd hoped for.

"I promise to work as hard as possible and make sure I leave Ross Academy a better place. But I can't do this alone. I'll need you to sign up for as many committees as possible, and join me, help me. Together, I know we will be able to accomplish great things. Thank you." With a nod, I sat back down to another round of applause.

David replaced me at the podium and went over the list of committees that would immediately need members, beginning with the pep committee. Dipak addressed the state of our treasury. Low. I resisted the urge to shoot a dirty look at Kevin Stroop. This, Dipak explained, could possibly extinguish my bonfire plans.

"Don't get me wrong," he said. "I think the idea is cool. But how are we going to pay for it? We'll need a permit, and to pay for the wood, and —"

"The permit fee would be waived," I explained. "I already worked that out with the local fire department." Of course I did. I wouldn't have suggested the idea if I hadn't thought it at least partially through. And I didn't appreciate the hint of condescension in Dipak's voice. But one thing I hadn't thought about was who would pay for the wood. "We'll just get a business to sponsor the bonfire," I said.

"I'm not sure that would work with Ross Academy rules," Ms. Bee said. "You know the board voted down the branded soda machines a few years back."

Spencer cleared her throat. "We could sell little kits to make s'mores and roast hot dogs. That would help offset the costs."

"That's a great idea, Spencer," I said. Seriously. I was impressed.

Dipak shook his head. "Offset is a good start. But we hardly have the collateral to begin with."

The room got quiet. I felt my good idea going up in smoke.

Autumn raised her hand. You didn't need to raise your hand at student council meetings, but Autumn so rarely spoke up, she probably never noticed. "How about you ask Connor Hughes? Maybe he could donate it."

I could have kissed her, it was the perfect solution. Connor's family owned the Hughes Christmas Tree Farm. They probably had plenty of scrap wood we could burn.

The rest of the meeting went smoothly. I took dutiful

notes and loved the way that all the people in the room found me, talked to my eyes. I was the focal point.

Ms. Bee looked surprised when Spencer raised her hand to be a freshman rep. And maybe it was a little bit overkill, but she also signed up for almost every single committee and group.

After the meeting, Ms. Bee asked if she could speak with me for a minute. She walked me over to the portrait wall, away from everyone else.

"I love the bonfire idea, Natalie. It takes me back to my Ivy League days. You're really thinking outside the box. And I'm anxious to see what other projects you propose this year."

"Thank you, Ms. Bee."

She leaned in close. "I didn't want to tell you this before, in case something terribly unjust happened and you didn't win the election. But there have only been eight other female student council presidents in the history of Ross Academy, and none since I returned to teach here eleven years ago. Which, honestly, as a woman who cares deeply about these sorts of things, made me feel like a complete failure."

I turned to say something, but Ms. Bee just stood there, admiring the wall and the rows and rows of slightly dusty frames holding the portraits of former student council presidents. It took a second before I realized her picture was right in front of me.

I knew Ms. Bee had divorced her husband — a professor of philosophy — several years ago. They'd lived overseas and had never had children. After the separation, she'd returned to her childhood home in Liberty River and begun teaching at Ross Academy.

She had been beautiful back then, too. Pin-straight raven hair, dark eyes, small pearl studs and a tiny gold cross. She was grinning more than smiling, one eyebrow arched with a tinge of mischievousness. *Nancy Bee.*

Ms. Bee pointed to the empty space next to the final picture, of Will Branch. Unfortunately, he'd blinked at the worst possible time. I wondered if people ten years from now might assume he was blind. "This is where your senior portrait will hang, Natalie. It's an exclusive club, but I know you'll make a wonderful member. And you'll be known forever as number nine."

It seemed, at the time, the best possible thing to be remembered as.

CHAPTER NINE

Everyone at Ross Academy had a school-provided e-mail address. I looked Connor Hughes up in the directory and typed a short message about the bonfire wood, asking him to please e-mail me back so we could discuss the details. I thought about giving him my cell number, too, but ultimately decided against it. I didn't need my number being passed around by those guys as a late-night drunk-dial prank destination.

He hadn't written me back by the next morning. I had checked every single period until lunch, when I spotted him at the cafeteria Ping-Pong table with none other than Mike Domski and a bunch of bottom-feeders like Marci Cooperstein.

Spencer clung to my arm. "There he is, Natalie. Go talk to him." We'd been collecting art supplies and covering the lunch tables with craft paper, in preparation for students to paint pep rally banners after school.

I would have preferred talking to Connor on his own, but I needed to know about the wood situation ASAP, since the success of my bonfire hinged on it. And I didn't want Spencer to think I was intimidated by the presence of Mike Domski.

"Maybe I should come with you." Spencer was all too excited about this possibility. "I'd give my left arm for a chance to chat up Connor Hughes. That boy is . . . ungodly hot. He looks like he's been raised on whole milk and fresh blueberry muffins."

Connor *was* good looking. It wasn't any one thing that stood out, but more like everything fit together in this smooth way. He had an easy way about him, like he didn't have a care in the world. He probably didn't, either. But Spencer and Connor? Or Spencer and any of those guys, for that matter? Bad idea. Terrible idea. "Go put these supplies in the closet and meet me back here," I told her.

Spencer looked disappointed as she tried to manage all the stuff I piled in her arms, but she did what I said. And, after a deep breath, I walked right up to Connor.

"Hey. Did you get my e-mail?"

Connor finished his volley, smacking the ball as hard as he could before turning to me. The force of it made my hair flutter. "Yeah, I got it. I'll drop the wood off Friday morning. No problem."

His voice was gravelly, like he had the beginnings of

a sore throat. And it didn't sound like it came from his mouth, but from somewhere warmer, somewhere deep in his chest. It seemed a little rusty, which would make sense, because Connor wasn't the kind of guy who talked much.

Mike threw the ball back at Connor, but it got stuck in the net. I grabbed it for him. "Great. I was worried that I'd have to come up with a backup plan. Everyone's really excited about the bonfire. It might end up becoming a new school tradition." I knew I sounded braggy, but I couldn't help myself from rubbing it in Mike Domski's face.

And honestly, I expected similarly pleased reactions from the rest of the people surrounding the Ping-Pong table. Not from Marci — that girl had it out for me. But the other football guys, because they were the ones who'd benefit most. The whole thing was practically being done in their honor. Only their faces were utterly stoic and unenthused. Mike Domski flicked his paddle at me, trying to get me out of the way, so the game could continue.

Except I didn't move. I stood still, because I knew it would make Mike mad. "Will the wood be here Friday morning?" I asked Connor. "Or later in the afternoon? I just want to confirm the details with you, so I can coordinate with the fire marshal and get this whole thing crossed off my To Do list."

Connor laughed. And not in the way where he might sympathize with how much time and effort it was taking me to get all this dealt with. He laughed like I was telling him a joke. "Consider me confirmed, RSVPed, and whatever." Then he threw his Ping-Pong ball up in the air to serve. But I guess he saw I was pissed, because he didn't hit it. He caught it instead. "Seriously, Sterling. I promise. You'll have the wood by homeroom."

"Dude," Mike said, in a fake whisper. "Natalie wants your wood. Bad."

Everyone snickered. Including the girls.

"I don't need anybody's wood. I can buy my own wood," I spat back, allowing my annoyance to clearly come through. It was only when everyone started cracking up that I realized what I'd implied. I walked away as fast as I could, and dreamed about a tragic accident where Mike's crotch caught fire.

CHAPTER TEN

The morning of the pep rally, I was too anxious to eat breakfast. Honestly, it was too early for breakfast. The sky was still dark when I picked Autumn up, and she slept with her head cradled by the seat belt on our drive to school. It was maybe a little type A obsessive of me, but I had involved myself in every last detail. I didn't want to leave anything to chance, not when the success of the entire pep rally fell squarely on my shoulders. Plus, I'd come up with a pretty ambitious design idea for the senior hallway. So for two full hours before school started, I worked harder than I ever had in my life.

Autumn stood precariously on the edge of a chair borrowed from Mr. Darby's Comparative Lit classroom. Grunting and stretching as far as her arms would allow, she lifted the edge of a twirled piece of blue crepe paper one centimeter at a time. "Do you want me to get a level?" she joked.

I ignored that, because I was stressed and because Autumn should have known how important this was to me, and checked my watch. We only had about fifteen minutes left to finish up. I ripped a piece of masking tape with my teeth and secured the corner to the wall. Then I cupped my hands around my mouth and called down the hallway. "Let's get balloons tied to every rung of the staircase, okay Carlie?"

Carlie Glaskov, dressed in her cheerleading uniform, manned the helium tank I'd gotten the supermarket to donate for the day. A bright-blue balloon stretched with helium, but instead of tying it off, she put it to her lips and sucked. "Got it, Natalie!" Her voice sounded like a cartoon mouse's, and she giggled so hard her face turned red. "Go seniors!"

"Go seniors!" I said back, a little frightened. "Watch her, will you?" I whispered to Autumn. And then I walked the length of the hallway, picking up stray pieces of tape, streamers, and popped balloons. About an hour before, a bunch of seniors who weren't in student council had shown up to help decorate. It was a real ego boost. Even some of the popular people, like Carlie. I knew she'd voted for Mike Domski, but she'd come anyway.

I got to the very end of the hallway, opened up the pay-phone booth, and sat on the bench inside. I stared down to the other end and took it all in. The senior hallway looked amazing, like a navy-blue-and-white candy cane. We'd striped every single inch of the hallway — the lockers, the floor, the ceiling. It looked like something right out of Willy Wonka or a fun house, just like I'd imagined. I couldn't wait for the rest of the senior class to see what we'd accomplished. But really, this would be nothing compared to my bonfire.

Dipak came bounding down the stairs. "Hey! How are the other halls looking?" I asked. I hadn't had a chance to check them myself.

Dipak pushed up the sleeves of his Ross Academy decathlon sweatshirt. "Well, us juniors have this whole feather motif going. We ripped open a bunch of pillows and dumped them all over the floor. But I'm a little concerned that it looks like we killed an eagle right there in the hallway. The sophomores are lame — they only have like two banners. But I was actually impressed with the freshmen. They made up fake newspapers with winning Ross Academy headlines on them." I smiled. Spencer had hinted all week that she had something special planned. "But no hallway looks as good as the seniors'," he said. "Like, not even close."

It was exactly what I'd hoped to hear. And now there was only one thing left for me to check on. "Did you notice if Connor dropped off the bonfire wood?" I asked.

Dipak shrugged. "I don't think it's here yet."

I tipped my head back. "I should have called him last night to remind him." I hated depending on other people. There was too much of a chance for them to let me down.

"You have Connor's phone number?" Dipak sounded surprised.

"No," I admitted, slightly insulted. Was it totally out of the realm of possibility that I would? "The Hughes Christmas Tree Farm is in the phone book."

Ms. Bee appeared in the hallway. She wore a navy A-line dress with gray leather pumps and several strands of thick white pearls, looking equal parts school spirity and expertly put together. I wondered — did someone like Ms. Bee even own a pair of sweatpants?

"Natalie, I've had such fun wandering the halls this morning. The school looks wonderful." She placed a hand on my shoulder. "I believe the fire chief is planning to come sometime between second and third period to take a last check of the bonfire setup before he signs off on the permit. Do you know if everything's ready to go?"

"We'll be good to go," I promised. At least, I hoped we would be.

A few minutes later, Autumn ran up. She pushed on my shoulders and pinned me against my locker.

"What are you doing?" I laughed.

"Painting your face!" she said, pressing the tip of a white grease crayon against my cheek. "You don't look school spirity enough for student council president."

I had been so busy with the preparations, I hadn't thought much about what to wear. I chose a plain blue sweatshirt, a pair of jeans, and my gym sneakers. I guessed it was kind of blah.

"Stop moving," she warned me.

"Nothing too big, okay?" I said, glancing at the feather that took up the entire side of Autumn's head.

"Shhhhh," she said.

I let Autumn paint me and enjoyed the buzz and fever and excitement in the hallway. I felt on top of the world until Martin came up and said, "Natalie, we have a serious problem."

"What? The wood? It's still not here?" I searched

around for Connor Hughes and started to panic. What if Connor never planned to bring the wood in the first place, just to make me look bad? What if this was a big joke made at my expense, because I'd beaten Mike Domski in the election?

Martin shook his head. "No. I mean, I don't know if the wood is here yet or not. But that's not the problem."

I stepped out of the way of Autumn's crayon. "What's the problem?"

"Nick Devito has the flu."

"So what?"

"So . . . there's no one to dress up as Ross the Eagle for tonight's game."

"Can't we get one of the freshmen reps to do it?"

"I can try. But a lot of those kids are on the freshmen teams or in band."

"What about Dipak?"

"Dipak has serious claustrophobic issues. He'd hyper-ventilate inside the costume."

"What about you?" I asked, my eyes narrowing.

"I'm supposed to be selling the merchandise at the game."

I took a deep breath. "Martin, are you telling me that I'm going to have to be Ross the Eagle tonight?"

He nodded solemnly. "Yes, Ms. President."

"Come on. Hold still!" Autumn said, grabbing my face and steadying her crayon. "Promise me you won't get this stressed out and miserable over every student council thing this year, okay? Everything is fine. The hallway looks great. Relax. Let's have fun!"

"Okay, okay," I said. She had a point. It was time to enjoy the fruits of my labor.

Suddenly, it was way too loud in the hallway. Connor Hughes and other seniors on the football team, dressed in jeans and their jerseys, headed to their lockers in a pack. Everyone cheered.

"Sorry, Autumn," I said, pulling away from her. "Give me a second."

The greasy crayon squiggled wildly to my earlobe, but I didn't care. "Connor!" I shouted as loudly as I could, trying to push my way toward him. "The wood?"

Connor turned around and looked confused, possibly at the blob on my face. Then he gave me a thumbs-up. The wood had arrived. Everything was going to be fine.

There was another noise. Music. A dancey song that I knew from the radio, only played faster and with more bass, growing steadily louder. The crowd suddenly parted. Autumn and I found ourselves pushed backward until we were pressed up against the lockers.

I stood on my tiptoes. Ten freshmen girls marched down our hallway in two lines, as if they were in a parade. They were led by Spencer. She had a pink iPod strapped to her bicep and she was holding two white portable speakers, one in each hand. She strutted like a model on a runway.

Autumn jumped, straining to see. "Doesn't she know that freshmen aren't allowed in the senior hallway on pep rally day?"

Of course, rules like that were ridiculous. You could go anywhere you wanted. Still, they were rules. And there seemed to be lots of them Spencer didn't know.

The girls had their hair up in ponytails tied with curls of white satin ribbon, and white terrycloth shorts that were way too short for any real athletic activity. I didn't recognize all of them, but I did spot Susan Choi, who was another one of my freshmen reps. Each wore the same fitted, blue, child-size T-shirt.

Murmurs and whispers overtook the cries of "Go home, freshmen!" as the girls strutted by to the beat. I heard laughter. Whistles. Catcalls.

I pushed forward to the edge of the crowd. Each shirt had a pair of bulbous footballs positioned like pasties over their boobs. And above them, the same single word was printed across the chest, curling in a perfect arch.

Rosstitute.

Autumn shook her head. "What the hell?"

The girls passed, and I noticed that underneath each swishing ponytail tip, the name and number of a varsity player was printed across the backs of the shirts.

Domski 27

Phillips 4

And on the back of Spencer's: *Hughes 14.*

Suddenly, it hit me. Like an SAT vocab word after breaking down the root.

Ross Academy + Prostitute = Rosstitute

The realization seemed to trickle out of my head and through the crowd. I saw delight on the faces of the football team and sneers on the faces of the cheerleaders.

Suddenly, the freshmen girls stopped on a dime. Spencer made the music go full blast. They changed formation, from two lines into a diamond shape, and then began to dance. Most of the girls looked painfully awkward. They were stiff and nervous, spinning at the wrong time, keeping their eyes on Spencer for cues.

Spencer was different, and I could definitively tell that, yes, she was a good dancer. She confidently made her way through the routine, keeping eye contact with people watching her, even though her curls were swishing in her face. Her moves were simultaneously precise and sexy as hell. She was the star of this show.

Ms. Bee reached out and grabbed Spencer by the arm. I had never seen her look so mad.

A few people actually booed Ms. Bee for stopping the dance. Mostly guys, from the sound of it. Ms. Bee looked around the hallway, possibly for me. I moved my head so it was behind someone else's. I was that embarrassed, and I didn't want to get involved. The hallway got quiet, except for the music. Everyone was watching what was going to happen. I felt like I couldn't breathe.

"These shirts are highly offensive, Spencer," Ms. Bee said. "Not to mention completely against school policy. You girls must change immediately."

It was almost like slow motion, watching Spencer grin. I only saw it for a second, before her face got covered up. Because she took off her shirt, right there, in the middle of the hallway. Her bra was a pink gingham number, with a tiny rosette in the center, underwire working overtime to hoist and enhance a modest amount of cleavage.

The grin returned, as a shirtless Spencer twisted the wad of material in her hands. "I'll turn it inside out, Ms. Bee," she said. "Problem solved."

The hallway erupted again. It was pure energy, and the freshmen were drunk on it. The other girls grabbed at the hems of their shirts, too. But before anyone else could strip, Ms. Bee had their leader by the arm and dragged her down the hall.

As Spencer passed me, she winked.

CHAPTER ELEVEN

"I honestly don't think it's going to rain," Autumn said, beaming her big smile up at the ominous sky, as if it could intimidate the storm clouds. "We just need to stay positive."

"I'm positive this sucks."

"Aren't you having *any* fun in there?" Autumn hid a smile by puckering her lips around the straw in her Coke. "I mean, you look awesome."

I rolled my eyes, forgetting that Autumn couldn't see my face through the small square patch of mesh. "As if this morning's Rosstitute parade wasn't humiliating enough, now I'm entombed in the bowels of a stuffed-animal carcass. Oh, and don't forget that all of the local weather reports neglected to mention the monsoon clouds threatening to obliterate my bonfire. This truly is the very definition of awesome. Seriously. Look it up and you'll find a picture of me."

Though the wind was steadily picking up, it was still hot and itchy inside Ross the Eagle. The oversize head smelled like the very bottom of a laundry basket, where the underwear that doesn't fit anymore, or the socks that have holes, stay unwashed for a long, long time. I felt like I was going to barf if I didn't get fresh air, so I tried to get my wings underneath the rim of the eagle head.

Autumn pinched my beak. "You can't take your head off on the sidelines! Look at all the little kids around! Remember how freaked out I was after we saw headless Big Bird smoking a cigarette in the Sesame Place parking lot? You're lucky I'm even standing this close to you right now."

"What's worse? That, or having Ross the Eagle die on the sidelines from heat stroke? Come on, Autumn. I'm so thirsty."

She guided the straw of her Coke through the mesh. "Here. The game's almost over anyhow."

Just as I sucked up some soda, the crowd behind us roared. Autumn turned away, taking the can with her but leaving the straw dangling out of my mouth. I spat it out.

"Since when do you like football?" I asked, spinning around to match the field up with the mesh window.

Connor Hughes lobbed a pass that fell out of Mike Domski's waiting hands. A ref blew his whistle and a Saint Ann's player tore off his helmet and screamed at his teammates until his cheeks turned purple. Connor sank to the ground and pounded his fists on his thighs. He was mad, too. Madder even. Though I didn't get why. We were winning twenty-one to nothing. He'd thrown all three touchdowns.

Our band kicked into the school fight song and I groaned. "How many times are they going to play this?"

Autumn patted me on the back. "It's showtime."

I shuffled the length of the sideline as mascot duty called for. I would have jogged to get it over with quicker, but the big yellow plastic eagle claws strapped over my sneakers made it hard to do anything fast. I didn't go the extra mile, like Nick Devito would, and ham it up for the crowd with cartwheels and pogo bounces and fist pumps. I basically just paced and flapped and prayed that the rain would stay away.

On the upside, with every lap, I got to check out the pile of wood. I had to admit . . . Connor had really come through. There was a ton of logs and branches from his family's Christmas tree farm all propped together in a big pyramid that was practically as tall as the snack shed. A group of firefighters in yellow reflective gear, heavy black boots, and helmets stood nearby. They split their time between watching the game and the sky.

As I reached the end of my lap, the floodlights turned on, and the last of the summer bugs swarmed in a fuzzy cloud under the glow. When I looked back down, I saw Spencer and her now-infamous pack of Rosstitutes returning to the bleachers, carrying trays of nachos. The punishment for their shirts hadn't come down yet; decisions and precedent needed to be considered.

As upset as I was at Spencer, it was hard to say what should happen. What they did wasn't as bad as fighting or stealing or defacing school property. But the punishment still needed to make a statement.

"I don't know why you're so mad," Autumn had said to me after the Rosstitutes had left the hallway. "This doesn't have anything to do with you."

Autumn was probably right, but it didn't make me feel better. More than anything, I was disappointed. After all, I'd tried. I'd tried to help Spencer in the bathroom that day, I'd tried to get her involved with student council, and she went and ruined all that goodwill. Not to mention completely stole the attention away from my hard work with the senior hallway. It was kind of infuriating, the sorts of things that got you noticed at our school.

I started to make my way back to Autumn when Spencer pointed at me and shrieked. The whole group of Rosstitutes veered away from the bleacher steps and surrounded me in a fit of giggles.

"Is that you in there, Nick Devito?" Spencer cooed.

I couldn't wait to tell her that it was actually me inside the eagle suit. I wanted Spencer to feel like a total idiot. I wanted to embarrass her, show her how ridiculous she was acting. But before I could get the words out, she grabbed one of my wings and started dancing, forcing me to be her partner. I stepped back, but Spencer stepped closer, grinding up on my leg.

"Don't be scared of me, Mr. Eagle!" she cried. "I won't hurt you."

As I wrestled to get away, I slipped on a bit of damp grass and nearly fell flat on my face. A few other Rosstitutes huddled around me, catching my fall. As I stumbled, I spotted Autumn a few feet away. She watched with stunned horror.

"Someone take a picture of us with the eagle!" Spencer cried.

I flapped my wings so they couldn't get too close, but the Rosstitutes closed in and pinned them to my side. I finally went limp just to get it over with.

"Make sure you zoom in nice and tight," Spencer instructed Susan Choi, who was holding the camera. Before they could get a shot, I heard our principal's voice booming from behind.

"All right! Settle down, girls! Go and have a seat." Principal Hurley waved his hands, dispersing the Rosstitutes. Principal Hurley was the oldest faculty member of Ross Academy. A bald man, stern and broad like an army officer, he wore a three-piece suit every single day. And he sounded more annoyed than I've ever heard him.

Ms. Bee walked over. "Are those girls causing more trouble?"

"I prayed that Martha and I wouldn't have daughters for this very reason." Principal Hurley sighed.

Ms. Bee looked up at the sky. "Well, if you care for my opinion, I think the ones who just wore the shirts should get a week of detention. But the ringleader, Spencer, I think we need to make an example of her."

"Three-day suspension?"

Ms. Bee nodded.

Whoa. Suspension. The anger I felt toward Spencer turned to pity. She wasn't a bad girl, just . . . misguided. A black mark like this on her permanent record might ruin her chance of getting into a decent college.

All because she'd done something so incredibly stupid. And for what? To impress Connor?

Principal Hurley nodded back. "I'll call them all into my office first thing Monday morning. I'd like you there, since this was partly a student council event."

"Yes. Of course."

I took off toward the fence, but Autumn was gone. I hoped she'd gone to get me a bottle of water or something. But I didn't want to stand there waiting by myself and risk getting accosted again. The only safe place was near the football team's bench.

As I shuffled over, a roar erupted from the home bleachers. Mike Domski had dropped another one of Connor's passes on third down. Our offense headed to the bench and defense took the field. Some of the lesser players tossed around plastic bottles and towels to the guys who had returned.

Bobby Doyle took off his helmet and stretched his arms over his head. "I'm ready for this game to be over." I've never seen someone stretch as often as Bobby Doyle. He wants to give people a peek at the Chinese characters snaking across his pelvis. He was so proud that he could get a tattoo without being eighteen, using his older brother's ID. I thought it looked corny, and I've heard most of those Chinese letterforms don't even mean what the tattoo places say they do. I wished I had a photographic memory. Then I could have researched them and told Bobby that his tattoos didn't mean *Strength and Courage*, but rather something ridiculous, like *Shiny Fat Rabbit*.

Mike Domski fake punched Bobby. "You wouldn't be so tired if you weren't such a tub of lard. You're only allowed to drink light beer tonight."

Bobby laughed. "Dude. Need I remind you that the party's at my house? And that the beer you're referring to, which is currently chilling on ice, is mine? And the hot tub, that I turned on at lunch to be nice and toasty, is also mine?"

Bobby Doyle's family was really rich, and had a separate guesthouse just for him. It was basically party central for our school, and it wasn't even nice, because he lived like a pig, with empty beer cans strewn all over the place and holes punched into the walls. Or at least that's what I'd heard.

"I just hope this stupid bonfire thing is over quick," Mike said. "Hey, Connor — please tell us you soaked those logs in kerosene." Connor shook his head. "Fine. I guess it's up to me to save us." And then Mike started to hop up and down. He slapped his hand over his open mouth.

A rain dance.

I clenched my fists. If the football team left early from the bonfire, I swore I'd make a huge scene. I'd throw Ross the Eagle's head right onto the fire.

Connor grabbed a protein bar from inside his duffel bag. "Come on, guys. The game isn't over. Can we please concentrate on the business at hand?"

"Tell you what. I'd like to make that Spencer girl's titties my business," Mike said with a laugh.

My mouth dropped open. Oh. My. God.

James Rocker squirted some water in his mouth, swished it around, and spat it back out. "She's not that hot."

Mike sighed. "Dude, it doesn't even matter, because she's *eager.* Did you see her dancing? I mean, she's practically a stripper."

Coach Fallon jogged over with his clipboard. "All right, we've got two more minutes. Second string, get in there and try not to screw up."

Connor looked like he still wanted to play, but ultimately he crashed on the bench and started pulling off his cleats without bothering to untie them first.

"Come on, Connor," James said. "Spencer had your name on the back of her shirt, lucky bastard."

Connor shrugged. "I thought that whole thing was pretty dumb."

I could hardly believe my ears. Connor and I actually agreed on something.

"Dumb, yes. But Spencer and those girls were trying to send us all a message. They *want* us," Mike said, matter-of-factly. "And if Connor isn't into Spencer, I'm next in line. . . ."

"She wants Connor, not you," James said.

"You think a girl like her will turn celibate because Connor shuts her down? Trust me, man. The Domski will make it happen. And none of you guys better try and cock block me."

My stomach rolled. The fact that Spencer actually liked Connor didn't matter. She'd made them all believe she was the kind of girl who'd take whatever she could get.

"Fine. I call the short one with the dimples," James called.

Connor laughed. "You have a girlfriend, dude."

James acted like he'd forgotten this. "Biggest mistake of my life. No one should have a girlfriend in high school. It, like, completely defeats the purpose. Mark my words. This time next week, Melanie and I are done."

I thought about poor Melanie Walsh in the bleachers, sitting next to James's mom. She practically worshiped

James, and always wrote him these long, detailed notes with four different color pens during homeroom.

Bobby looked off into the bleachers, shielding his eyes from the floodlights. "That skinny blond freshman would be cute if she weren't totally flat. I might as well feel up my little brother."

James joined him. "I'd pick her over Mindy Polchek." Mindy was a sophomore. Her dad worked at the same architecture firm as my mom. "I mean, Mindy does gymnastics and shit. But you still have to look her in the face."

I wished that I could have had a tape recorder on me, so I could show Spencer and those girls exactly what the guys they desperately chased after really thought of them. The Rosstitutes were just sluts, girls to use and cast aside.

"What about Sterling?" Bobby asked.

My entire body burned a thousand degrees. I didn't want to hear what they had to say about me. I didn't want to hear their jokes, their put-downs. But I couldn't move. I had to listen.

Mike Domski stuck out his tongue and made gagging sounds. "She's the kind of chick who'd cut off your balls in the middle of the night. Wait, actually, I wouldn't be surprised *at all* to hear Natalie Sterling has a bigger dick than I do."

I wanted nothing more than to walk over and give Mike Domski a kick between the legs. Only it was more embarrassing to let the guys know that I'd been standing there the whole time, listening to them say all these disgusting things.

"She has a decent face," James said.

I crossed my wings smugly. But really, what was I doing, feeling proud about some weak compliment? And who did these guys think they were, judging *me*? I wasn't like Spencer. I wasn't putting myself out there to be looked at, evaluated. I wondered how they'd like it if I talked about Mike Domski's overly hairy arms, or how James was so short that any girl who wanted to take him to a dance would have to wear flats, or the chicken pox scars dimpling the back of Bobby's neck.

Connor lifted his head and made a scrunched-up face. "Whatever, man. You're still mad that Sterling kicked your ass in the election. And threw that pizza bomb at you, which was classic. That girl is seriously tough. I wouldn't mess with her."

I felt a swell of something inside of me. Maybe it was shock, or pride, that Connor Hughes defended me.

Just then, there was a huge crack of thunder, the kind that echoes in your chest. Some of the girls in the bleachers screamed. A second later, the sky opened up, pouring rain fast and hard. In a matter of seconds, my costume was soaked through. All I could think about was my bonfire. I had to get something to cover the wood, or else my first big act as student council president would be washed out.

I tried to run, but I slipped on the grass and fell hard, right on my back. The whole crowd said *Ohhh*. I tried to get up, but it was totally impossible. The ground was too slick and the costume stuck to me like a straitjacket.

I felt a pair of hands hoist me up to my feet. "Careful there, Devito."

I turned and there was Connor. And I swear he looked through the mesh window and saw it was me.

"You okay?" he asked quietly.

I wanted to say yes. And thank you. But I was also completely mortified by what I'd just overheard. I ripped my arm free and hobbled toward Autumn, off in the rainy distance.

Her hair was saturated, stringy, and sticking to her face. I watched her shimmy halfway up the woodpile, trying to get a blue tarp stretched over the top. She was fighting a losing battle to keep the wood dry, an army of one. No one else helped her.

I ran up and extended my hand. "Come down. It's not safe."

"I've almost got it. Run over on the other side and I'll —"

"Autumn, forget it. There's no way we're still having the bonfire." Even though I knew this was the truth, it still hurt to admit it.

Autumn tipped her head back and rain splashed off her cheeks. "Are you sure? I think it might be slowing down."

Another crack of thunder shook the air.

I grabbed Autumn's hand, helped her down, and together we took off running for my car.

The whole ride home, I had the chills. Not because I was soaking wet. Because the bonfire was ruined, because Spencer was an idiot, because I was so upset and disgusted by what I'd heard, because Connor may have caught me eavesdropping.

I told Autumn about the terrible things I'd overheard, only leaving out what Connor had said about me, since that wasn't the point. I knew the way the guys talked about the girls would make her upset, but I still wanted her to know. If anything, it would keep something like last weekend's party incident from happening again. These were not the kinds of people we should be associating with. Autumn knew exactly what those girls were in for. It put a heavy silence over the car.

But how could I get it through Spencer's thick skull that she was making some really bad choices? And the rest of the freshman girls, too? I wished there was a way I could help them like I'd helped Autumn.

"It's too bad we can't take every girl in school to the young women's conference Ms. Bee told me about. But it's all the way in Boston, and it's not until spring break."

Autumn turned her head. "What if you held your own women's summit? Like, at school?"

It made immediate, total sense to me. "Autumn — you are a genius! I could basically replicate the entire thing. Lectures, discussions. We could run it together."

Autumn bit her nails. "I'll help you in any way I can, Natalie. But I really don't want —"

That's when I told Autumn about that first day of school. About my ideas for changing freshman orientation. Autumn would be our guest speaker. She'd have a chance to stand out again, this time for something good. For something positive.

Autumn looked down at her chewed-up fingernails. And then she said, "Can I ask you something? Without you getting mad?"

"Okay."

"Did those guys say anything about me?"

I shook my head. "No." It was the truth, and I thought that would make Autumn feel good. Except it didn't. She rested her head against the window with a deep sigh, and dragged her finger through the condensation in one long, sad streak.

There was something severely wrong with the girls I knew.

CHAPTER TWELVE

It rained the whole weekend, and by Monday morning, everything felt damp and bloated. The ground shimmered with slick fallen leaves, and thick mist hung in the air like the curtains on my bedroom windows. I pulled my hair back and walked across the lawn, grass squishing underneath my loafers, wetness seeping through the cracks in the leather, soaking the toes of my knee socks. But it didn't even bother me. I couldn't wait to get to school. I was on a mission.

After the homeroom bell, I headed straight to the main office and sat on the bench outside Principal Hurley's office. Most of the Rosstitutes were already there, waiting to hear their fate. The secretary called them in one by one.

None of the girls made eye contact with me, except for Susan Choi, who managed a meek smile, which I did not return. She hid for the rest of the time behind a hefty paperback of *The Lord of the Rings*.

Susan seemed like a nice girl. Quiet, studious, and obsessed with J. R. R. Tolkien. I noticed she always had her paperback open in her lap during student council meetings. Not the kind of girl you'd expect to be a Rosstitute. Spencer clearly had a strong, magnetic quality about her. I had felt it even when she had approached me in the bathroom. Intervening felt like a necessity. Who knew what this freshman Pied Piper could do if she really hit her stride?

Spencer arrived last, seconds before the first period bell. I heard her voice before I saw her, laughing and squealing from somewhere down the hall. Then she appeared, running as if danger were in hot pursuit. But she moved like she didn't really want to escape.

As soon as she saw me, the smile dropped off her face.

"We need to talk," I said.

"Don't you have to get to class?"

I hoped I could get a pass from the secretary. But even if I couldn't, if I got in trouble for sticking my nose in where it didn't actually belong, it still felt worth it. "For you, Spencer, I've got time."

Spencer shrugged and sat on the bench next to me. "I know you're probably mad, but I didn't do anything wrong."

The defiance in her voice took me by surprise. I expected remorse, or at least some fear about her impending punishment.

"You were in your bra!" I couldn't help but say. "In the middle of the hallway!"

"I was not. That was my bathing suit, not my bra. The bathing suit I wear during first period swim class."

Her excuse took a little wind from my sail, but I stood strong. "Those shirts were really gross, Spencer. A prostitute? For the football team? Come on."

"They were a joke!" She waited for me to be convinced. "Okay. Look. The hallway probably wasn't the best place to change out of my shirt . . . and for that, I guess I'm sorry. But I still think people are making a big deal over nothing."

My stomach tightened. If Spencer tried to explain herself like that to Principal Hurley and Ms. Bee, she might just get expelled. "You should work on a better apology ASAP. One that actually sounds sorry. Do you know how much trouble you're in?" My eyes bounced all over her face. "Big trouble," I hissed. "Humungous trouble!"

The office door opened, and Susan Choi exited. Her glasses were up on the top of her head, and she dabbed at her red eyes with a wrinkled-up wad of tissue.

I imagined Susan had never so much as gotten a B before, never mind a week's worth of detention. I gave Spencer the eye, like *See? This is serious.* But Spencer had her compact open and was patting powder on her T-zone.

The secretary peered around the doorway and called for her.

"You don't have to worry about me," Spencer said sweetly, rising to her feet. "I can take care of myself. I swear." She did not expect me to stand up and follow her, but that's exactly what I did. "Natalie," she whispered over her shoulder, "what are you doing?"

"I'm saving your ass," I said, and pushed past her.

I had only seen the inside of Principal Hurley's office once before, when I was called in, with the rest of the academic decathlon team, to take a photo for the newspaper with our trophy. Being there, even under positive pretenses, still gave me an uneasy feeling. The air in his office felt like August, thick and uncomfortably warm. The cinderblock wall had been painted a creamy beige, probably in the hopes of making what constituted a prison cell feel slightly more homey. He had no plants, no pictures, no decorations other than a huge vintage Ross Academy banner, made of moth-eaten wool and with hand-stitched, yellowing letters.

Ms. Bee stood in the corner, leaning against a set of tall filing cabinets. She looked surprised to see me.

"This is a private meeting," Principal Hurley said.

"Yes, Natalie," Ms. Bee added. "Stop by my office later. We'll talk then."

I ignored them both and sat in one of the overstuffed leather chairs facing Principal Hurley's desk — a gutsy move, for sure, but I needed to appear confident.

"Principal Hurley. I have something to say." He laced his fingers and nodded for me to go ahead, probably against his better instincts. "What happened on Friday was terrible. The behavior of these freshmen showed extremely poor judgment. But instead of punishing and isolating the girls involved, I think you're missing the chance to make this into a real learning experience, something every girl in our school could benefit from."

Principal Hurley looked over at Ms. Bee, not exactly sure what to make of this. She had the tiniest smile on her face. "Go ahead, Natalie," she said.

"The female population of Ross Academy is clearly focused on the wrong things. They value boys' attention over their own accomplishments. They're content with being objectified. The T-shirt incident was exactly that — a desperate attempt to be noticed, to proclaim subservience. It's as if our girls don't understand that they can be recognized for other things — their goals, their brains. Not just their bodies." I feared that I sounded too rehearsed, because I *had* rehearsed. At least ten times, to my bedroom mirror. But I needed Principal Hurley to take me seriously. I wanted him to know I had thought this through. I pulled the pamphlet Ms. Bee had given me out of my book bag. "I'd like to lead a seminar that would be mandatory for the girls involved in Friday's incident, but also open it up to any other girls at school who might like to participate."

Principal Hurley's face curdled. "An assembly? That hardly seems like a fitting punishment."

I had to think fast. "I was actually thinking more of an overnight shut-in. We'd do workshops and discussions and get people to sponsor each of the hours we stay awake, which we'd donate to a women's shelter or something. It'd be a Girl Summit, an empowerment symposium."

"A what?" Spencer asked.

I shot her a look. "I think that, for most of us, this would present an opportunity to discuss the recent events and maybe learn better behaviors and strategies moving forward. Instead of sweeping Friday's incident under the rug, we'd open up a dialogue about it. I want our girls to know that they are more than a sexual commodity, that they should have larger goals and aspirations for themselves."

Principal Hurley dropped his head to the side. "And you are willing to take this all on your shoulders? Why?"

I had not anticipated this question, and suddenly, I had a hard time organizing my thoughts. I thought of Autumn and all she had gone through. I looked over at Spencer, who was clueless. I cared so much about these girls. And if I could help save them, or anyone else at school, from making a huge mistake, I gladly would.

"Because this is important to me, Principal Hurley. And I won't be doing it alone. I'd like to run it with Spencer. For better or worse, Spencer showed real leadership on Friday, and I'd like to give her the opportunity to use that for good. And the extra responsibility, in addition to perhaps a week's detention, would make a fitting punishment, since she was the ringleader of the whole Rosstitute incident."

Spencer gazed over at me. Despite everything, she actually looked flattered by my compliments.

I saw Principal Hurley working it over in his head as he stared at me. I stared right back. I knew that if I wanted to do this, I'd have to show some strength.

Ms. Bee looked like she might explode with pride. "I think this is a wonderful idea, Principal Hurley. Senior year is extremely busy, and yet Natalie's offering to carve out time to help guide the girls of Ross Academy to a more beneficial path."

"Fine," Principal Hurley said with a sigh. "This is a little unconventional for my tastes, but so long as Ms. Bee agrees, we'll try your seminar."

Outside the office, Spencer cornered me immediately. "For the record, I still don't think I did anything *that* bad."

"For the record, you were about to be suspended."

She put her hands on her hips. "I'm not as stupid as you think I am. I know what I'm doing."

I suddenly remembered a few hissy fits Spencer had thrown, in my babysitting days. I'd found that the best way to deal with her tantrums was to turn my back and walk away. So that's exactly what I did. I marched down the hall, and I didn't turn around when she started whining my name. Spencer was worse than a bratty little sister. But that didn't mean I couldn't get her to listen.

First period had already started, so I hustled down the hall to the AP Chemistry lab. When I rounded the corner, I saw Connor Hughes leaning into the water fountain.

Part of me wanted to backtrack and take another staircase, so I wouldn't have to pass him. A nervous energy buzzed through my chest. I still wasn't sure if Connor realized I'd been inside the Ross the Eagle suit, if he knew I'd heard the things they'd said. But purposefully dodging him would give Connor far too much power over me. So I kept walking, one foot in front of the other.

He looked up from the stream of water. I saw this out of the corner of my eye, my senses heightening the way they do when someone's watching you. I became instantly conscious of my gait (borderline scampering), my body temperature (overheated, from Principal Hurley's office), and my breath (cottony and stale).

Once I had passed, he said, "Hey, Sterling — aren't you going to thank me?"

I couldn't completely ignore him, because that would appear too calculated. So I stopped. The classrooms around us all had their doors closed. We were alone.

"For what?" I sounded defensive. Accusatory. More so than I had planned. But even though he'd said some nice things about me at the football game, he had far from earned a free pass.

"I got up early and loaded all that wood back into my truck so you wouldn't have to deal with it." He held up his hands. They were rough and slightly dirty. "The logs were really wet and slippery. I got a couple splinters, too. Deep ones. They might just cost me the next football game."

So Connor went out of his way to do me favors all of a sudden? I could hardly believe it. I felt myself starting to blush, so I pulled the elastic out of my hair and let it fall like a cloak.

"You moved all that wood by yourself?" I asked.

"Nah. I forced some of the JV kids to help me."

"Well, I didn't ask you to do that."

"I know you didn't," he said, a split between annoyed and amused. "I felt bad that your little thing got rained out."

My little thing? "I didn't need your help," I barked. "I would have handled it."

He pulled both hands through his hair. It still looked wet from his morning shower. "Geez. I was only looking for a *thank you*."

"Well, you know what, Connor? Here's an important lesson. You can't always get what you want. Even boys like you." I left him standing there, as baffled as he probably was in his remedial math class, and grinned at the empty hallway stretching in front of me. I was sure Connor had never been treated that way by a girl before. As with most things in life, it felt extremely good to be the first.

CHAPTER THIRTEEN

At the end of the week, Ms. Bee called me into her office to discuss my progress on the girls' night. I wondered if Spencer should be part of the conversation, too, but ultimately I decided against it. There was something important, something personal, I needed to ask Ms. Bee.

We'd just finished a student council meeting. There were a lot of big projects on the horizon, like the fall flower sale and the Halloween dance, for which I would need a costume. I hadn't worn one since I was twelve and dressed as double helix.

Ms. Bee hung up her red cashmere sweater on her coat rack. I sat down in the chair across from her desk and looked around.

A picture album sat on her desk, the kind that had a photo in the front — in this case Ms. Bee sitting on a sandy-colored rock wall, overlooking the most beautiful ocean I'd ever seen.

"Barcelona," she told me. Her summer vacation. I was surprised when she opened the book and let me flip through, as she narrated her trip. Suddenly, Ms. Bee became less like a teacher, and more like the kind of cool aunt who could talk your mother into letting you order a glass of red wine at a fancy restaurant.

She pushed her hair back and fingered a pair of dangly, hammered gold earrings. She told me she'd haggled a man from ten euros down to three at an outdoor bazaar. And when rain moved in, evidenced by a sky that grew dark then black in the photos, she fled to Milan on a whim. "When you travel alone," she explained with a wink, "you are free to be unpredictable."

I bounced up and down in my chair and told Ms. Bee that's exactly how I planned to backpack through Europe next summer, before college started.

Ms. Bee nodded, and her approval felt as good as a hug. We talked countries, possible stops along the way. I took out my notebook and took diligent notes. It was also the perfect segue.

"Ms. Bee, I was wondering if you'd consider writing me a recommendation letter for my college applications. I know it's only October, but I wanted to get a jump on things."

She smiled. "Of course, Natalie. In fact, this helps me a great deal. I can't tell you how inundated I get with these kinds of requests come March. Some students give me only a week's notice. If everyone could be as responsible and considerate as you, my job would be a lot easier. Not to mention that it's been a complete pleasure having you in my classes and working with you in student council. So yes, I would be honored to write you the most glowing recommendation in the history of recommendations."

"Ms. Bee. I can't thank you enough for all the help and attention you've given me this year. Really."

She leaned back in her chair, and her eyes drifted off my face to just over my shoulder. A big, expectant smile bloomed on her face shortly thereafter. "So, tell me. How are things coming with your girls' night?"

Truth was, it was slow. I'd had a ton of homework that week, not to mention cramming in as much SAT prep as I could. But I tried to dress it up. I had figured out which charity the donations would go to, and made a list of the food and snacks I'd have to buy.

Ms. Bee still seemed pleased. "I want to help you." She started pulling books off of her shelf. "You should read *The Feminine Mystique*. And of course *The Beauty*

Myth, which will be highly relevant to your discussions. Oh! Flip through *The Woman's Bible*. And *The Second Sex* — I based my master's thesis on the work of Simone de Beauvoir."

As the books piled high on the corner of her desk, I tried to look excited, but really, I felt completely overwhelmed. I guess Ms. Bee could tell, because she furrowed her eyebrows. "And Spencer, she *is* helping you, correct? That was part of the deal."

"Yes," I lied. I mean, I knew Spencer would help me. We just hadn't had time to sit down with each other yet. Really, if that was anyone's fault, it was mine. I was the busy one.

"I'm concerned because I've seen Spencer flitting around school, happy as can be with all the newfound attention she's brought to herself. That is not the attitude of someone who regrets her behavior. Frankly, I'm at a loss as to why you've chosen to take someone like her under your wing."

I felt embarrassed. Why did Spencer make this so difficult on herself? "I babysat Spencer a long time ago," I explained. "So I guess I feel some responsibility for her. She's definitely making some stupid choices. But she's a good girl, deep down."

If Ms. Bee understood me, she didn't show it. "Wait! I forgot the most important book of all." She went to her shelf. "This one is just for you, Natalie." I took it from her hands, unprepared for its weight. A girl graced the cover, smiling into the wind, a leather cap and goggles perched on the top of her head. The title was *East to the Dawn: The Life of Amelia Earhart*. "I devoured this over my vacation. I think you and Amelia have a lot in common. Have you heard of the Ninety-Nines?"

"No."

"Well, Amelia founded the Ninety-Nines as an organization just for female pilots. In fact, she became its first president. It helped legitimize the women who pursued such nontraditional careers, providing them with opportunities. Strength in numbers and all that. It completely reminds me of this girls' night. And, of course, I found the significance with the number nine all too fitting."

"Thank you, Ms. Bee."

"I'm proud of everything you're trying to do here, Natalie. I've always known you were special. Other girls your age, well . . . they get so silly over the boys. You, my dear, are fiercely independent. You've got a good head on your shoulders, and frankly, you give me hope that feminism won't die off with your generation."

I smiled and pulled my book bag up onto my shoulders. It weighed about a million pounds. Though, honestly, it felt nothing compared to the pressure behind Ms. Bee's smile.

CHAPTER FOURTEEN

The following week, Spencer and I arranged to meet before school to finalize our plans for the girls' night and get our sign-up materials prepared. Autumn came, too.

I divided up the readings from Ms. Bee between the three of us, with the instruction that we should look for inspiring quotes or messages we could give away to girls in the hall on slips of paper, like the ones in fortune cookies.

Spencer bit the end of her pencil. "Natalie, do you have a boyfriend?"

Autumn laughed, which pissed me off. I didn't like Autumn hinting at my inexperience, and giving Spencer more opportunities to lord her expertise over my head. Anyway, it was none of Spencer's business.

"No, I don't," I said proudly. I thought for a moment how I could have shocked both Spencer and Autumn if I told them how Connor had been paying me attention. Ever since the bonfire night, I'd caught him watching me. Not that I cared. He was free to look at whomever he wanted. And I was free to ignore him.

"I bet you only date college guys." Spencer drew hearts instead of bullet points in her notebook. "Some completely brilliant boy who's going to be a neuroscientist or a foreign policy adviser. He probably wears glasses, but not nerdy ones. The thin metal kind that models wear. Ooh! And I bet he's from somewhere overseas, like London. I could totally see you with a guy who has an accent."

I put my pen down. "I'm not discussing this with you," I said. But if I'd wanted to date anyone, he would have been exactly like the guy Spencer had just described. Except not from London. Paris. And we would have spoken French to each other. After all, I'd been studying it for three years of high school. It had to come in handy for something.

"How about you, Autumn?" Spencer went on. "Do you have a boyfriend?"

Autumn's eyes went to the table. "Oh, me? No."

I shot Spencer a look to quit it, but unfortunately, it didn't register. She turned her chair so that it faced Autumn. "Okay, that makes absolutely no sense. I mean, Lisa Prince has a boyfriend, and she's practically got vampire teeth. But you . . . you're one of the prettiest, nicest girls at this school. I don't understand how you aren't, like, a shoo-in for Prom Queen."

"I . . . sort of have a history."

"What do you mean?"

Autumn and I shared a grimace. Autumn didn't want to be my guest speaker at the girls' night, and I had to accept her decision. Still, a part of me hoped Autumn might open up to Spencer.

Autumn took a deep breath and closed the book in front of her. "Do the words *Fish Sticks* mean anything to you?"

Spencer looked utterly perplexed. "Umm . . . a disgusting food made only slightly less disgusting by ketchup?"

Autumn smiled. And then she told Spencer her story. She said it frankly, almost without emotion. It was strange how controlled she suddenly seemed to be about the whole thing. Spencer was the exact opposite. Her smile sank lower and lower and lower.

"So the last guy you were with . . ." Spencer's question hung in the air.

Autumn bit her lip and nodded. "It's fine. There's no way I'd have the grades to get into a good school if that whole thing hadn't happened. I'm probably better off. I mean, I know I am." Autumn sounded only half-convinced. I gave her arm a friendly pinch to make up the difference.

Spencer had a different take on things. "No!" she cried. "Autumn! That's probably the worst thing you could have done. You shouldn't let one dumb guy make you feel bad about yourself. And closing yourself off from guys is completely unnatural. I mean, why else would teenagers be swimming in hormones if we weren't supposed to use them?" She gritted her teeth. "We should go hunt down Chad Rivington and cut off his balls."

I shook my head. Spencer was missing the point. Big time. "There's not a single guy in this high school good enough for Autumn. For any of us, really."

"Oh, I know I'm too good for any guy at this school. But that doesn't mean I can't still have fun with them in the meantime. Because what college guy is going to date me? Hello! I'm only fourteen, and I'm not looking to shack up with some pervert."

Autumn cracked up. "I don't think that's what Natalie meant, Spencer."

Spencer still wasn't getting it. I knew I had to pull out the big guns. I closed my book and turned to face her. "Look, I never told you this because I didn't want to hurt your feelings, but I overheard Mike Domski and the other guys saying some pretty nasty things about you after the Rosstitute incident."

"Natalie," Autumn warned me.

At first, Spencer didn't seem fazed. "Oh, yeah, like what?"

"Well . . . someone called you a stripper. And I think James was the one who said that you weren't even that pretty. After Connor made it clear that he wasn't interested in you, Mike claimed he'd easily get you to do stuff with him, and said none of the other guys could touch you."

I watched it all register on Spencer's face. It was one thing to hear what happened to Autumn, but there was no playing this off. I'm sure it was hard to know what people were saying about her behind her back, but my hope was that it would finally make her understand that how she was acting was just bringing trouble.

"Unbelievable," she said. "*That's* why Mike Domski's been practically stalking me. He's always walking by my locker or bumping into me by accident. If he thinks for a second that he can lay claim on me, he's got another thing coming."

This, I felt, was the right attitude to have. "Look. We've got to get cracking if we're going to get everything ready for sign-ups. We've only got about an hour."

After we finished up the quotes, we made a list of activities for the girls' night. I'd gotten most of them off the internet and from the pamphlet Ms. Bee had given me. It felt like things were coming together.

"We're missing something," Spencer said, shaking out her curls. "Something essential."

I gave our list a quick rundown, but it seemed good to me. "What?"

"*Fun*, Natalie! There's absolutely nothing fun on this list!"

I pointed to number six. "What about the trust falls?"

Spencer made a goofy face. "You want this to be full of girls from school, right? Well, then we need to give them a reason to spend Friday night with us, rather than having a good time somewhere else."

I wanted to tell her that the girls' night was less about fun and more about learning, but Autumn cut me off. "Spencer's right," she said. "It can be educational, but we need something entertaining, too."

Spencer twirled a curl around her finger. "I've got an idea."

I sighed. Deeply. Then again, Spencer actually wanted to be involved. I knew I should encourage that. "Okay. Shoot."

"Well, we used to do this thing at my old dance studio. We called it Sweatpants Dance. We'd invite all the girls to the studio for a dance party. But *only* girls. No boys allowed. Everyone would show up in sweatpants and tank tops. And you didn't have to worry about guys or looking good. One of the girls would DJ and we'd play corny, embarrassing boy-band music and everyone just danced it out together for a couple of hours. We could do the same thing, only in our pajamas. Plus, we could kill a bunch of time that way."

Autumn clapped. "I love it!"

They both turned to me, to hear what I had to say. I smiled. "It's a great idea. Spencer, you're a genius." Which was a little much, but I wanted to be encouraging.

In response, Spencer surprised me. "I just want to say sorry for what happened on pep rally day," she said, her tone suddenly serious.

"You don't have to apologize to me," I told her, and was happy that it felt true.

"Yeah, I do. Because of my stunt, we've been forced into this punishment."

"This isn't a punishment," I clarified. "Suspension is a punishment. This is a summit, a chance to —"

"Whatever you want to call it, I'm sorry. And, Natalie, I really do appreciate what you did in Principal Hurley's office. Standing up for me like that."

"That's what friends do for each other." It was the first time I'd said those words to someone other than my best friend, but I meant them just as much.

We set up a table in the main hallway with a sign-up sheet, and a bunch of literature and inspiring quotes by female leaders. Spencer insisted on making her iPod play pop songs sung only by female artists. A nice touch for sure.

People started showing up for school and a bunch of girls stopped by our table right away. The big draw seemed to be Spencer's Pajama Dance Party idea, but a few girls seemed to really like the quotes Spencer and the rest of the Rosstitutes handed out, too. In about fifteen minutes, we had thirty girls sign up. It was going really, really well, until Mike Domski grabbed a pencil and tried to add his name to one list.

"Put that down," I told him. Honestly, you had to talk to Mike like he was a three-year-old.

"Why? Shouldn't boys be allowed, too? If you exclude us, isn't that sexist?" I tried to take the pencil back, but he pulled it away. "Oh, I get it. This girls' night is more of a vaginathon. No dick allowed."

I wanted to spit back some biting retort, but Spencer beat me to it. She put her hands down on the table and leaned into Mike's face. "That's right, Mike. No dicks, no dickheads, no cocks, no penises, no wieners, no wee-wees, no boners, no dongs, no dill weeds, no scrotums allowed. Which, I think, are all adjectives used to describe you." She yanked the pencil right out of his hand. "So, yeah. Looks like you're not invited."

Mike's response? He gave Spencer the finger and walked away.

"Point: Spencer," I whispered, and drew a line in the air.

"Trust me. I know how to deal with guys like Mike," she said. "In fact, I think I'm going to break him. Just for fun. Just because I can."

I threw my arm around her. Not because I cared about what kind of psycho mind games she could play on Mike Domski, but because Spencer was finally listening to me.

CHAPTER FIFTEEN

There's no way Spencer actually wears that to sleep.

That's what I thought, anyway, when she appeared in a navy-and-green-plaid baby-doll nightgown, with white ribbon trim where the hem grazed her thighs. Her wool coat hung open, belt ends skimming the gym floor, as if she'd worn a party dress too pretty to keep under wraps. It could have maybe passed for one, if not for the pillow puffing out from under her arm and the sleeping bag dragging behind her.

"Natalie!" she squealed. "I made the most awesome playlist for tonight!" She did a little shimmy out of her coat, which caused one of the delicate spaghetti straps to fall off her shoulder. "Got me checked off, right, Ms. Bee?"

"Spencer Biddle," Ms. Bee recited from her folding chair, her pencil scratching against a clipboard. "How could we have missed you?" I felt like Ms. Bee had made the joke for my benefit, but really, I couldn't laugh.

Spencer scurried over to meet up with the rest of her friends. There were about fifty girls present, plus the Rosstitutes and a few other student council girls that I guilted into coming. I had hoped more would have signed up, but I guess Mike Domski scared them away with his disgusting jokes. Still, it was a halfway decent turn out.

"All right, Natalie," Ms. Bee said, "I think you can get started. I'm going to be in my office for a while, catching up on some paperwork. Plus, I think if I'm not around, the girls might be more inclined to open up and discuss things."

"Great. I'll grab Spencer and —"

"Natalie, I'd like you to be more of the facilitator tonight. I know Spencer helped in the planning, but this is your wonderful idea. And you have the leadership experience. I don't want tonight devolving into some tittering sleepover. You've got actual, important work to do."

I nodded. "Sure. Of course."

I walked across the gym to where everyone was mingling. It felt strange to be in pajamas at school, especially because, unlike Spencer, I wore what I actually slept in. My dad's old hospital scrubs used to be maroon, but they'd turned a lighter pink, having been washed so many times. I also had on a white tank, an oversize hooded zip-up, and my slippers.

I paced the bleachers and gave the girls a chance to quiet down. "Okay. Hey, everyone, thanks for coming tonight. We've got a lot of snacks and munchies that we'll tear into later, but I wanted to go over a few things first." I took a deep breath, and made sure to smile. That's when Spencer stepped right in front of me.

"I have a statement I'd like to make, before we get started. I want everyone to feel like this is a safe place for us to talk about what's been going on, to share our feelings and thoughts. This should be a judgment-free zone."

I smiled over at Ms. Bee, who headed out of the gym. "Of course, Spencer. That's a great point." I pulled Spencer close and whispered, "Why don't I get things started and then you can take over?" Spencer looked confused. And maybe a bit wounded. I nudged my chin toward an empty seat in the bleachers. "Don't worry."

Spencer sat next to Autumn. Begrudgingly.

"I think the perfect place to begin tonight is to discuss what happened in the senior hallway two weeks ago." I'd barely finished before Spencer's hand shot straight up. I stared over her fingertips. "I expect lots of you have different thoughts and opinions and I want to make sure we hear from everyone." Spencer started bouncing on her butt, waving her hand wildly. The more I tried to ignore her, the harder she tried to be noticed. "Spencer? Why don't you start us off?"

Spencer stood up and faced the crowd. "I have to say, I felt shocked by people's reactions to the T-shirts. I mean, why aren't girls allowed or encouraged to show their sexuality?"

"I don't think what you were doing was sexy," I told Spencer as gently as I could. "You were trying to get attention."

Spencer smiled. "See? That's what I mean. That's what we should be talking about tonight! Boys can mess around and do whatever they want to without consequence. But not us girls. We're not allowed to have sexual needs."

"Sexual *needs*? Are you serious? You're fourteen."

"I don't know what my age has to do with anything." Spencer pursed her lips. "I'm sensing a lot of negativity coming from you, Natalie. Isn't this supposed to be a judgment-free zone?"

"Okay, let's all calm down." Which sounded ridiculous, because Spencer and I were the only ones getting heated.

"Look, I don't do things I'm not comfortable with. I am *always* in control. And anyway, what right is it for anyone else to tell me what I can and can't do with my body? I won't be villainized because I happen to like being sexual. I'm not going to be embarrassed. It seems that this school has a real problem with that sort of thing." Spencer gave a pointed look at Autumn, which everyone noticed. "Forcing girls to be ashamed for doing the things that come natural to them — it's a ridiculous double standard, and we should all, frankly, tell anyone who judges us to screw off."

A couple of girls nodded, including Marci Cooperstein, who was sitting directly behind Autumn. I watched as Marci reached out and gave Autumn's shoulder a little squeeze. Autumn turned around, surprised. The two girls smiled at each other. And I wanted to throw up.

Melissa Sanchez raised her hand and Spencer called on her. "My brother found out I gave a hand job to one of his friends, and now he won't even look at me." Her chin started to quiver.

"See what I mean?" Spencer said. "That's horrible! Because I bet your brother wishes a girl would give *him* a hand job. But because you're his sister, you're dirty."

I caught Autumn's eye and mouthed *help*. After all, she was sitting next to Spencer. If she could grab her hand and pull her down . . . do something. Autumn saw me. I knew she did. But all she did was look up at Spencer and smile.

My control was slipping away. I quickly announced, "Now that we've got that out of the way . . . let's start tonight off by breaking out into groups. I've put some women's magazines out on the tables. I'd like everyone to tear out any positive female images and negative female images they see."

Everyone broke into groups. Spencer marched over to me. "Why do you shut me down every time I open my mouth? I was making good points out there."

I dragged her near the doors, out of earshot. "Listen, I'm sorry if you felt I cut you off. It's just we have a lot of things planned for tonight and a pretty tight schedule. I do want you to feel like you've got a say. But I need you to follow my lead, okay?"

Spencer narrowed her eyes. "Aren't we supposed to be doing this together?"

"Yes, but you need to voice your opinions in a way that's beneficial to the group. No one wants to see the two of us arguing."

Spencer threw her hands up. "Fine, Natalie. Whatever

you want. You call the shots. And I'll just stand here and be your bad-girl prop."

"That's not what's going on." I folded my arms. Why was Spencer making this so difficult? It wasn't all about her.

"Well, it sure feels that way," she snapped.

"Look, you can lead the next discussion."

"Whatever," she said, then stormed off.

I couldn't believe it. How was it that Spencer didn't see the enormous olive branch I'd just handed to her?

"What's happening?" Autumn asked. "Why are you being mean to Spencer?"

"I'm not!" I ran my fingers through my hair. "Spencer's making a mess of everything. I could have used your help out there, except you were too busy making up with Marci to notice. Seriously. What was that about?"

"Honestly, I have no idea." Autumn sounded genuine. "But I thought this was what you wanted tonight to be."

I sighed, because Autumn couldn't understand. She didn't have Ms. Bee breathing down her neck.

After a few minutes, Spencer called everyone back to the bleachers. I stood right next to her, so I could intervene easily if she got out of line.

"Let's start with this picture." Spencer held up part of a back-to-school pictorial, where a sexed-up vamp of a teacher stood on her desk in fishnets and stilettos, with schoolboys cowering in a pile on the floor. "Does anyone have any thoughts?"

No one raised their hand, so I stepped up. "I find this picture pretty sexist."

"Really?" Spencer asked.

"Umm, yes. This woman is clearly being objectified."

"But don't you think she has the power in this situation? The boys are literally throwing themselves at her feet, groveling for her attention."

I stared at the picture. Maybe Spencer had a point, but I still said, "Not really."

"See — that's exactly what I mean. Any woman who dares show her sexual power — well, we automatically assume she's being victimized, taken advantage of. When really, we're the ones in charge."

I pressed my lips together tight. When did the topic of the night become how Spencer had the right to slut it up?

Autumn raised her hand. "What do you mean, exactly?"

Spencer smiled wryly and began to offer advice to the girls. "It's about confidence," she said. "You have to know who you are, what you want, and then use your feminine powers to make boys give it to you."

I groaned.

"Come on, Natalie. Haven't you ever felt wanted? Had a guy stare at you so hard, he forgets to blink?"

I shrugged my shoulders, even though I had. With Connor. But it wasn't something I felt in control of. It was something I tried to ignore.

Spencer went on, talking about how great it is to be in control of your sexuality, and to use that power to make guys worship you. Michelle Heller told everyone how she'd gotten a guy to buy her a prom dress because he wanted her to be his date that badly. Spencer had the rest of the girls give Michelle a rousing round of applause.

I found a seat in the bleachers and pretended to read some article in one of the magazines no one had bothered to pick up. I was so mad, I couldn't see any of the words. Just the white space in between the lines.

I realized there was no changing Spencer. I was stupid to try.

CHAPTER SIXTEEN

Someone shook me awake. "Natalie?"

I opened my eyes and saw Susan Choi kneeling over me. "Yeah?" I asked in a sleepy voice. I wasn't sure what time I fell asleep, but it didn't matter. Technically, it was my job to make sure at least one girl stayed awake through the night, so we'd earn the donations for our all-nighter. Except Spencer had basically railroaded my entire evening. She DJed the dance party, while I cleaned up the food. She organized a makeover session with everyone's collective makeup, leaving me to pick up used cotton balls and Q-tips. And she held an impromptu photo shoot of girls in their pajamas, for which I was not invited to pose, but to juggle fifteen different cell-phone cameras.

I tried my best to maintain some semblance of control when Ms. Bee came back into the gym, but once she went to lie down, I climbed into my sleeping bag out of protest. Not because the girls' night wasn't a rousing success — it was. But I shared no part in it.

"I think Spencer let some of the football boys in the school," Susan whispered.

I shot up, fully awake. Other sleeping bodies lay around me, including Autumn, who shared my pillow. "What? When?"

Susan made the *shhhh* sign. "Just a few minutes ago. I saw Spencer leave first, and then more girls slipped out of the gym one by one."

"Where's Ms. Bee?"

"She's asleep on the couch in the gym office. You'd better get them out of here before she wakes up, Natalie. We'll all be expelled!"

I wanted to roll over and let Spencer get in trouble. But I knew I couldn't. If Ms. Bee found out about this, she'd never respect me again. Not to mention Principal Hurley. If I screwed this up, there was a real chance I'd get suspended right along with Spencer.

The hallways were dark, save for some emergency lights mounted near the stairwells and the blue glow of computer monitors and television screens not turned off for the weekend. It felt scary and dangerous, like a horror movie. I passed through the math wing, moving as carefully and quietly as I could in my slippers, following the laughter and playful screams from the science labs around the bend.

Shadows flickered across bulletin boards and rows of lockers, silhouettes of people running around. I turned the corner. A bunch of kids disappeared down the stairs. One large figure, definitely a boy, ducked into the girls' bathroom halfway down the hall. Three girls chased after him.

I kicked off my slippers and sprinted toward them as fast as I could, my bare feet smacking the floor. The sound of my pursuit only made them laugh and scream louder. I grabbed one girl by the straps of her cami and pulled her to a stop, even though I feared the whole thing might tear away in my hands.

"Hey! Careful!" she squealed, all excited and flushed at having been caught. Her face fell when she turned and saw me.

"Go back to the gym," I told her as sternly as I could. "Right now." I prayed she would actually listen to me.

The other two girls stopped and gave me sour looks. They were all Rosstitutes. One opened her mouth to say something, but I stared her down until it snapped shut.

"Do you really want to get in any more trouble than you already are?" I asked.

The three of them walked dejectedly back toward the gym.

I turned back and pulled the bathroom door open.

The moon shone brightly through a window, and it gave off just enough light to see Connor Hughes perched up on the radiator in jeans, a worn flannel shirt, and a dark green canvas jacket. He did not expect me to be the one who followed him inside, and he actually looked a little bit scared.

"What are you doing here?" I hissed.

Connor jumped down. "I forgot a book I needed."

"Save your ridiculous excuses. You guys need to leave right now, before we all get expelled."

"Come on, Sterling. We're just having some fun."

I watched him work his moves. The way he stood, so relaxed and casual, the way he smiled at me out of the corners of his mouth. He was confident, completely sure of himself. In that moment, I understood the true power of being a guy like Connor. He could probably talk a girl into anything. Except there was no way he could talk me into not throwing him out.

"Connor, I'm serious. You either leave now, or I'm getting Ms. Bee."

"You wouldn't do that," he said, stepping toward me.

I laughed. Did he expect me to faint or something? I took a step toward him, folded my arms, and leaned in. "Oh, yeah? Try me."

We stared each other down like that for a second,

and a strange feeling came over me, starting warm at my toes and spreading up through my body.

"I like your PJs," he said.

"Shut up," I said.

He grinned. It made one dimple appear on his left cheek, which looked sandy with stubble. "You're pretty tough, aren't you, Sterling?"

I liked that Connor called me by my last name. Some girls might have been insulted, because that was more how boys talked to each other, but to me, it was a compliment. And so was the word *tough*. I wanted to believe that he meant it. He'd said it before, that time on the football bench. But I couldn't figure out why he was telling me now, except to sweet talk me out of waking Ms. Bee. I needed to show Connor that I wasn't going to fall at his feet like the other girls at school. So I took another step forward and put my hands on my hips.

"You have no idea how tough I am," I said.

He took another step. A big step, closing the gap of air between us.

And then he kissed me. He grabbed me and kissed me, and his whole body tensed up. It was a bold move, kissing me without asking first.

I couldn't let him get away with it.

So when I felt him pull away, I leaned forward and kissed him harder, camouflaging my inexperience with enthusiasm. This kiss had heat behind it. There was no need to ask for permission. It absolutely had to happen.

When we pulled apart, my heart was beating insanely fast. I wanted to kiss him again. But instead I summoned up the words and said, as sternly as I could, "Now, do what I say. Get out of here."

That's when he finally took a step back. I relished the space and felt my body temperature go down. "Okay," he said. Then he walked out.

It took me a few seconds to move. When I left the bathroom, Connor was at the end of the hall, rounding up the other guys, telling them, "Let's go. We're out of here."

Behind me, I heard a door open. I spun and saw Mike Domski slip out of the science lab and run to catch up with the boys. He had a big dumb smile on his face.

"See you later, Natalie," he called, mocking.

I took one last lap around the school and made sure all the hallways were clear. When I came back into the gym, I saw Spencer lying in her sleeping bag with her eyes closed. She was faking, but I didn't say anything.

One moment filled up my whole mind, my whole body: I, Natalie Sterling, had just kissed, and dismissed, Connor Hughes. I felt a strange peace carrying this humongous secret, because I knew that nobody in the gym would believe it. I couldn't even believe it myself.

CHAPTER SEVENTEEN

"Can I talk to you for a second?"

Spencer practically accosted me at my locker on Monday morning. "I want you to know that I didn't invite those guys to the school. They just showed up. I was trying to get them out. I wouldn't do anything to get you in trouble, Natalie." She put her hand over the Ross Academy crest on her sweater vest. "Swearsies."

I kept my eye on Spencer. She seemed to be telling the truth. "Did Ms. Bee say anything to you?"

"No. Why? Do you think she knows?"

I had my suspicions. Ms. Bee had been a little cold to me the morning after the sleepover. She seemed way more interested in finding hot water for her tea than in talking to me. Hopefully, her crabbiness had been because she had a bad night's sleep on the gym office couch. "I don't think so."

"Good. Then everything's okay." Spencer smiled. "It was kind of exciting, right?"

It was. Kind of.

◎ ◎ ◎

I began to see Connor way more often. Or maybe I just noticed him more. But after that night in the bathroom, we tended to run into each other a lot.

It turned into a game we'd play, in the halls, at the office, in the cafeteria. Connor would look at me and grin, this knowing grin full of mischievousness and secrets, and I'd flat out ignore him.

One time, we bumped into each other in the parking lot after school.

His frame bulged with his football pads, since he'd just finished up with practice. I had stayed late, working on the Halloween dance decorations and waiting for Autumn, who'd left a book in her locker. Most of the cars that had parked between ours that morning had pulled away, leaving just him and me.

"Hey, Sterling," Connor said. He sat on his bumper and poured Gatorade down his throat, past the lips I had kissed. Despite the grass stains and sweat and dirt, he still looked good.

I didn't respond. I could have gotten in my car, but that wouldn't have been fun. So instead I put my books, one by one, in my trunk.

"You coming to the game this Friday?"

I turned to face him and had to shield my eyes from the setting sun. "Why would I do that?"

"Because I'm playing," he said, puffing out his chest. "And anyway, isn't that part of being student council president? You know, to support the athletic teams?" He smiled, thinking he was well on his way to making a convincing argument. It was kind of adorable, really. Because Connor obviously had no clue that I was one of the top debaters at Ross Academy. No matter how he tried to argue his point of view, I was always, always going to have a comeback.

"That doesn't fall under my job description. Sorry." I said it real sarcastic.

"We're four and one this year. We've really got a shot at the playoffs."

"Good luck with that," I deadpanned.

He stood up and walked a few steps toward me. "Come on. Come to the game."

I slammed my trunk. "I'm sure you have enough adoring fangirls in the stands." I tried to be smooth, only I dropped my keys on the ground. When I straightened back up, Connor stood practically on top of me.

"But I don't like them." His eyes held mine and his voice had a funny sound to it, as if he were talking and groaning at the same time. I couldn't exactly tell if he was teasing me, or if he was embarrassed by what he'd just admitted.

Either way, I burned. I burned a thousand degrees.

I heard one of the heavy metal school doors swing open. Autumn. My heart caught in my chest. "I have to go," I said fast, and ducked under Connor's arm.

He must have seen Autumn, too, because he didn't say anything more. He just walked back toward his car.

Finding a good Halloween costume proved more of a challenge than tracking down the Holy Grail. And for a place that billed itself a Halloween Superstore, the selections were pathetically limited.

"I hope we find costumes that work together," Autumn said.

"Me too," I said, and thought of Marci Cooperstein. Now that the two of them had buried the hatchet, I wanted to make sure Marci didn't get any ideas. Autumn was *my* best friend, and I wasn't going to let Marci weasel her way back in. Autumn forgave her, but that didn't mean they could pick up where things had left off before the whole Fish Sticks thing.

Autumn said, "It's kind of crazy that we've never

gone to one single dance together. I mean, it's not like we're homeschooled or something."

Autumn's breakup with Chad had happened right before the Halloween dance, when we were freshmen, so of course we avoided it. The following years, it seemed like a weird anniversary, remembering everything that had happened, so we'd always done our own thing.

"I wouldn't get too excited about this dance," I said.

She got pouty. "Why?"

"Well, I don't want you to set yourself up for disappointment. I mean, how great could a school dance really be? We're still going to be in the gym, where we've all sweated and done crunches, and it smells like feet. Not to mention that running a dance is a TON of work, on top of all my regular obligations."

"You are such a downer, Natalie."

Ever since the girls' night, Autumn had been acting different. Happier, I guess. I knew I should have been glad about this. But for whatever reason, it gave me a bad feeling.

"I don't see any adult costumes," I said, turning the corner on another aisle. "Everything's for kids."

"Not everything," Autumn said. She stood in front of a beaded curtain and pulled her hand across it, as if it were an oversize guitar she could strum. Pink fluorescent light poured out from the room. I followed Autumn inside.

"Okay," I said warily. "I think you found the adult section."

Autumn looked over the racks. "So are you looking for something more of a French maid, or maybe . . ." She started laughing so hard she could barely breathe.

"What?" I asked.

She pulled a rainbow colored tube dress from off the rack and held it up to herself. "Slutty clown? Who would buy this?"

I bit my finger. "Ringling Brothers says I'm a very bad girl!"

We spent the next ten minutes cracking ourselves up over these stupid costume choices, which were either confusingly slutty or completely androgynous. A bunch of other shoppers got annoyed. In their defense, we were being really loud. Only I didn't care. It felt like old times, when Autumn and I could be silly with reckless abandon.

I wasn't any closer to finding a costume, though, and that pissed me off. "Great," I said. "So I can either be a whore nurse or some disgusting cow with big plastic pink udders."

"Wait a minute. This one is actually kind of cute." Autumn held up a dress shimmering with blue and green and white iridescence. It looked a bit clingy, but at least it was long — stretching all the way to the floor.

"Game-show hostess?" I guessed.

"Nope." Autumn plopped a long blond wig on her head and wrapped a black shawl around her shoulders. It was a loose net, with plastic pink starfish and green sea horses glued on. "It's a mermaid costume! What do you think? It's cute, right?"

"Autumn . . ." I didn't know how to finish. Honestly, I shouldn't have had to finish. It was so apparent.

"Okay," she said in a sour voice, and hung it back up. "Never mind."

I felt terrible, but why was Autumn trying to make me feel bad for pointing out the obvious? What kind of friend would I be if I let Autumn wear that costume, especially since she was so desperate to have a good time at the dance? It'd be like walking into the lion's den wearing a suit made of steaks. "Forget this place," I said. "Let's make our own costumes. It'll be fun."

"But you're so busy with student council stuff," she pointed out. "You won't have time. We've barely hung out since the election. And the dance is next week."

I was annoyed, because this was my very concern in September, and was why I'd wanted Autumn to think about being vice president with me. But it was too late for any of that now. "I'll make time," I told her. "I promise."

"So what should we be? Can we still try to make the joint costumes work?"

I said yes. And I meant it — at least until we were on the way out of the costume shop, and I saw a brown, fake leather pilot's hat and a pair of big black goggles. I knew immediately: I wasn't going to be slutting it up or dumbing myself down this Halloween.

I was going to be Amelia Earhart.

CHAPTER EIGHTEEN

When I stepped though the doors of the gym on Halloween night, I could hardly believe how awesome it looked. I mean, it had looked good when I'd finished decorating after school, but everything was way better in the dark. The bleacher railings were covered in spiderwebs. The cardboard gravestones we'd made last week actually appeared real in the low light. Pumpkins cordoned off the dance floor from the rest of the gym, and the DJ we'd hired brought lots of flashing lights and a smoke machine. The whole room was misty. You couldn't see the lines on the floor or the gym mats or anything.

Autumn came running up to me. "You're finally here!" I couldn't believe my eyes. Autumn was wearing the mermaid costume from the Halloween shop. Before I could even come up with something to say, she wrapped me in a big hug — well, as much of a big hug as she could manage, considering that I was standing inside a cardboard airplane that hung from my shoulders by a pair of twine suspenders. "Your costume looks amazing, by the way. I can't believe you made it."

"Not without a price." I held up my hand and showed Autumn how raw the sides of my fingers were from cutting through the cardboard with a dull pair of scissors. Aside from my injury, I loved my Amelia Earhart costume. I had on the cream-colored silk blouse I bought to wear for college interviews and a pair of brown pants tucked into my leather riding boots. I'd curled the ends of my hair and pinned it all up so it looked like a bob. And the pilot hat and goggles looked great. But the plane made moving around a little unwieldy — I should have made my wingspan a little less broad.

"I ran out of time to make something," Autumn admitted, looking down at her slinky gown.

"Oh." I didn't know what she wanted me to say. She already knew I thought it was a bad idea.

Autumn leaned in close to my face. Her eyes got wide. "Do you have makeup on?"

I shrugged my shoulders — Autumn's excitement embarrassed me. "Just lipstick. Amelia would have worn it, so I borrowed a little bit from my mom for authenticity's sake."

It wasn't true. Amelia was known to be almost androgynous. But I'd enjoyed putting on the cherry red color and then carefully blotting my lips on a square of toilet paper, leaving a kiss behind. I'd never worn lipstick before. Burt's Bees, sure, but nothing so dramatic. I couldn't help but wonder if Connor would notice.

"I can't believe all these people are dancing," I shouted over the pulsing music. A big mob of kids undulated up and down together.

"I know! And it's not just the girls. Even some of the football guys are out there."

So the football boys had come. I wasn't sure if school dances would be "cool enough" for them. They were probably just there for the hoagies. I wanted to see what Connor's costume was, if he'd even bothered to dress up.

Autumn took my hand and dragged me away from the wall and deeper into the gym. I looked around, but because of the lights and the smoke and the costumes, I had a hard time making anyone out.

"Do you want to get something to drink?" I shouted over the music.

She nodded, and together we walked over to the refreshment table. That's where all the teachers were standing in costume. Principal Hurley looked totally appropriate in army fatigues and shiny black lace-up boots.

The only teacher without a costume was Ms. Bee. And even though it made everyone else around her look kind of stupid, I felt a little sad for her. Like for some reason, Ms. Bee couldn't dress up, even if she wanted to.

Her eyes lit up when she saw me. "Oh, Natalie! I absolutely love your costume. Promise me you'll let me take a photo with you before the night is over." Her smile dropped to a frown as her eyes went over my shoulder. "I only wish other girls would follow your lead. Principal Hurley and I discussed the possibility of imposing a costume dress code for next year's dance."

I turned and saw Spencer. I'd sort of expected her costume to be over the top, and, sure enough, she had transformed herself into a slutty construction worker. But her costume didn't look cheap and plasticky, like the kind of prepackaged outfits they sold in the back room at the Halloween shop. It was well made, obviously one of her dance costumes from an old routine. It dawned on me that Spencer's closet was probably a Halloween treasure trove.

Her outfit consisted of a skintight little denim minidress cut to look like a pair of overalls. She had a tight white cami on underneath, and the whole thing fit her like a corset, her boobs bubbling up over the top. The skirt stopped right underneath her butt cheeks, and when she dipped and bent to the music, you got flashes of a pair of electric orange booty shorts. A cropped mesh vest, reflective orange, hung over her shoulders like a shrug. She had on a hard hat, and a tool belt full of plastic toy tools. And — who knows where she got these — it was all topped off by a pair of Timberland-style lace-up high-heeled boots.

She really, truly, looked like a stripper.

And she really, truly didn't care.

She danced between two of the football players. One was Mike Domski, dressed in a black-and-white striped jailbird outfit, with a broken set of handcuffs twirling around his wrist. You could tell Mike was totally into Spencer. He wouldn't take his eyes off her. And the other guy making the Spencer sandwich, Paul Zed, didn't even have a costume on. Just an enormous Afro wig. Both boys pressed against Spencer, squeezing her in between them. She looked like she was having the time of her life.

Behind them, I noticed Dianna Berry, a girl in my AP French class, dressed in a plaid bodice, white stockings, and stacked penny loafer heels, puffing on a pipe. I laughed so hard I almost spit out my Coke.

After Autumn and I were out of earshot of Ms. Bee, I said, "Is Dianna supposed to be Slutty Sherlock Holmes?

Oooh! I'll solve that mystery . . . and then give you a lap dance! Seriously. I would have thought she was better than that."

"Dianna's a nice girl," Autumn said.

I shook my head. "What does that have to do with anything?"

"She's just having fun." She said it like her words were loaded. Like we hadn't made those same jokes at the costume shop last week.

It occurred to me that maybe we were having some kind of secret conversation. Like this wasn't about Dianna at all. "Look at her," I said. Dianna tugged on the back of her skirt as she swayed to the music, trying to keep her butt covered. I mean, Dianna was a pretty girl, and supercurvy. But her costume hugged in awkward places. It pinched around her arms and the zipper wrinkled up instead of lying flat down her back. She looked much prettier in her school uniform, I thought. "Does she look like she's having fun? Or does she look like she desperately wants some guy to pay attention to her?"

Autumn wrinkled her nose. "Are you going to act like this the whole night?"

"Act like what?"

"Nothing. Whatever. I just want to have a good time."

"Me too," I said. I didn't understand what was going on. Autumn practically tackled me when I walked in, and now she was trying to pick a fight with me over Dianna's costume.

And then I noticed Connor Hughes, also in a prison outfit, watching Dianna dance.

My heart dropped. A bunch of guys were sitting on top of a tall stack of floor mats. Bobby Doyle whispered something in Connor's ear, but whatever he said wasn't interesting enough for Connor to pull his eyes off Dianna.

I wanted to look away, but I couldn't. Of course guys like Connor were going to notice the scantily clad girls dancing in front of them. I mean, how could they not? It was practically instinctive. Primordial. Immunity to booty and boobs did not occur in teenage boys. But I felt completely stupid for putting on lipstick tonight. It made me feel as desperate as Dianna and all the other girls. It made me hate myself for even trying. Because, really, I knew better.

When the song ended, Dianna limped over to the bleachers, slipping off her very tall heels as she went.

Connor's eyes moved off her and roamed around the gym.

They stopped on me.

I took a deep breath and looked past him at some invisible person in the crowd. I wanted his eyes to stay on me. Hold me, the same way they had held Dianna. But I only kept his attention for a second. Barely a second. In fact, I couldn't even be sure if he'd noticed me at all. It happened that quick.

A terrible feeling formed in the pit of my stomach. Had I imagined things with Connor? I mean, yeah, we'd kissed, but he kissed girls all the time. Maybe it had been a dare. Or maybe I was a terrible kisser. I hated how I felt. Stupid. Insecure. Used.

Another song came on. Everyone cheered. Autumn, too.

"Come on, Natalie! Let's dance!"

"I don't know this one." I reached for a napkin and rubbed at my lips.

Autumn grabbed my hand. "Neither do I. But that doesn't mean we can't dance to it!" She started moving to the music, swinging my arm to the beat. It was almost more embarrassing than actually dancing.

I pulled my hand free. "I think I'll just hang out here.

The table's a little messy. Plus I feel bad about being late. I should help out."

"Please!" Autumn begged, trying to grab my arm again. "Dance with me!" I took a step back and she got all frowny. "Come on. I don't want to leave you here standing all by yourself."

"I'm fine," I told her. "Go ahead."

Autumn gave me a look. She knew me too well. I wanted to tell her about the whole Connor thing, but I couldn't. Not with her in that weird costume. Not with some crappy rap song on full blast.

"Whatever," Autumn snapped, picking up the fishtail train of her sequined dress and walking away.

Marci Cooperstein was already out on the dance floor, dressed as some kind of go-go-dancing crayon. She was waving her hands for Autumn, and when Autumn ran over, they practically jumped into each other's arms. They started dancing, spinning each other around and doing some funny choreographed moves that they were clearly making up on the fly. I tried not to be jealous, but I was. I was bitterly jealous.

I immediately busied myself, making sure all the snacks were out, that we had plenty of ice in the cooler. Over my shoulder, I heard the rest of the kids scream every time a new song came on. It made me feel so incredibly lonely.

When I ran out of chores to occupy me, I watched Spencer. Her moves were so smooth and confident, even if she looked totally ridiculous in her costume. She didn't just dance with one or two guys. She danced with the entire school — boys, girls. Everyone watched her, Connor included. I saw him. Despite my best efforts, every time I tried not to look at him, that's exactly where my eyes seemed to land.

At a break between songs, Spencer headed over to the snack table, followed by her pack of friends. Her forehead sparkled with sweat. She reached for a can of Sprite from the cooler and held it to her cheek.

Her friends went off to the bathroom, to check their hair and makeup. Spencer walked over to where I was standing and smiled at my costume. "You look so . . . classy," she decided, which made it seem even more wrong for the night. I tried to turn away from her, but I hit her with one of my wings. Spencer peered inside my cardboard plane and bit her lip, like she was debating whether or not to tell me something. "You know, Natalie, you have such a good body. Your butt looks totally hot in those pants. Why are you hiding it from everyone?"

162

I didn't like the feeling of Spencer checking me out. It made me feel small, even though I was taller than her. "I'm not hiding anything."

"Well why aren't you dancing? Do you need me to teach you a few quick moves in the hallway?"

"I'm fine. But thanks." I sounded anything but thankful.

"I seriously don't get you." Spencer twisted around and leaned against the table, pushing her boobs out. "You could get any guy in this room, if you just loosened up a little."

"Thanks for the advice," I said, annoyed. Because I had the guy everyone wanted. Only I didn't anymore. "Looks like you've got Mike Domski tangled up in knots."

She smiled. Smug. "Too easy."

"Just be careful," I pleaded. But Spencer didn't hear me. She was already bouncing back to the dance floor. And what did she need to be careful about, really? She was having a fabulous time. She got the attention she wanted. And I had neither of those things.

Connor walked across the gym toward where I was standing. Before I knew what I was really doing, I stepped out of my cardboard plane and kicked it underneath the table. And then I started fixing stuff that didn't really need to be fixed, just for something to do.

I heard him come up behind me. It was almost too easy.

"Hey, Sterling," he said. "You having fun?"

I laughed. "Not as much fun as you. I've seen you drooling over every girl in the gym."

"So you've been watching me?" He winked, all coy and cocky.

My voice caught in my throat. "Don't flatter yourself."

"Why are you so mean to me?"

I said, "Because I don't trust you," which was true. And as much as I knew that, the rush I felt when I had Connor's attention still made me feel drunk. I was acting crazy, and I didn't think I could control myself. I didn't even want to try.

He didn't say anything else, so I kept my back to him and dumped a bunch of M&Ms in a bowl. He reached for one almost immediately. At least, I thought that's what he was reaching for. But his hand stopped just short of the bowl. And when he opened it up, I saw a slip of paper in the center of his palm.

I turned around to face him. "What's that?" I asked, even though I knew. I knew, but I couldn't believe it.

"Nothing," he said, and that's when I smelled the beer on his breath. "Why don't you see for yourself?"

"I'm not taking a dirty piece of paper out of your hand," I told him.

"Sterling." He laughed at first. And then, when he saw I wasn't kidding, he groaned.

I stared him down. How dare he groan at me! Like I was so impossible? His eyes were all sleepy and soft, but his cuteness could not dilute my anger. "Why don't you give this to one of the slutty girls you've been watching. Like, I don't know, Spencer. She had your number on her stupid Rosstitute shirt. I'm sure she'd be okay with fooling around with you tonight."

"Just take it."

I crossed my arms, so Connor put the paper inside my pocket. His hand warmed me like a hot little coal, and when he pulled it out and reached for some M&Ms, I was sure the whole bowl would melt.

His smugness made my stomach flip over. "Here." I pulled the paper out of my pocket and tried to give it back. "I'm not interested."

Connor stepped toward me. Since I didn't have my plane on, he could get really close. Close enough that I saw he'd shaved, and had a tiny cut right where his chin met his neck. Close enough that I could smell the plastic of his costume. He took my hand and folded it over his number, to make sure I held on to it. He did it just like a magician, sneaking a red foam ball into his hand for a trick. And then he walked away.

I unfurled my hand and saw the paper. It was no trick. And I knew what had just happened. Things could have only gone so far when we were flirting in the hallway, or that night in the bathroom. But Connor had raised the stakes. Suddenly, it was my move, or game over.

CHAPTER NINETEEN

After the dance ended, it was the student council's job to make sure the decorations were taken down and the leftover food was cleaned up. Most of the students were already gone. Just a few people stuck around, and I was the only one really working. Coach Fallon led me around, pointing out all the stepped-on candy corns and sticky spots on his gym floor. I wanted so badly to tell him that it was his beloved athletes who had decided to throw candy at each other, whose bumping and grinding had sloshed the soda out of their cans. Not me. Not the girl who had to clean up everyone else's good time, like Cinderella.

Autumn sat in the bleachers, talking to Marci and a few other girls. I was pissed that she wasn't helping clean up. The longer I had to stay here, the longer it would take before we could get back to my house. I was exhausted, and I could only imagine how tired Autumn felt. Once she'd left me to go dance with Marci, she hadn't stopped until the last song. She'd ignored me practically the whole night.

After Connor left the dance, I kept touching the piece of paper in my pocket. Like I needed to make sure I hadn't dreamt the whole thing up. Because he walked right past me on his way out the door, without a second look. I guessed I really did embarrass him.

"Hey," Autumn said, coming up behind me. "A bunch of people are going out to Bobby Doyle's house."

"Yeah," I said. "So?"

"So . . . I'm going to stop by there for a little while. Do you want to come?"

"I thought you were sleeping over." I could hear the hurt in my voice. I hated it.

"I still am. I'm just taking a slight detour first. For an hour, tops."

It wasn't even an invitation. It was an ultimatum.

I looked over her shoulder at Marci and the other girls. They watched the two of us, somewhat impatiently. I was obviously holding up their evening, only I didn't care. I wasn't going to make this easy for Autumn. So I turned and started walking away from her, toward the supply closet. Autumn followed, but slowly, like a child being dragged through a department store.

"I don't get it," I said, once we were out of view of

everyone else. "Marci Cooperstein was a complete bitch to you, and now you're ditching me for her to go to some party full of jerks who've made fun of you." Even if a part of me wanted to go, I couldn't. Connor was in all likelihood going to be there. I didn't want to make it seem like I was suddenly chasing after him, or whatever it was that Autumn was chasing after.

"God, Natalie! It's just a party. And I'm not ditching you. I want you to come." Autumn dropped her head back. "Marci apologized, and I forgave her. It's over."

I pulled open the supply closet and chucked the broom inside. "I'm going home," I told her. "You can do what you want."

And that's exactly what Autumn did. Without even saying good-bye.

An hour later, I pulled into our driveway. As I walked toward the house, I crammed my cardboard airplane into one of the trash cans. Amelia Earhart had crashed and burned.

Mom and Dad were in the living room. Dad was asleep, Mom curled up in his arms. "How was the dance?" she whispered. And then, glancing behind me with a bit of surprise, she asked, "Where's Autumn?"

"She felt sick," I lied, and headed upstairs.

Cardboard scraps and art supplies were all over my room. I didn't want to bother cleaning them up, so I threw everything in a pile on the floor, shut off the lights, and climbed into my bed.

I lay awake, picturing Autumn at the party. I wondered if she was having fun. She probably was. I bet Marci was making sure of that. She wasn't going to let this opportunity slip by. She was probably talking about me, telling Autumn she'd done the right thing by leaving me behind.

As mad as I was at Autumn, I still worried about her. Despite the fact that she'd basically broken my heart, I hoped that Autumn wouldn't get made fun of by anyone. Lord knows that Marci wouldn't stand up for her. I put my cell phone next to my pillow, just in case I got a teary phone call from her. So I could be there for Autumn, like I always was.

I closed my eyes. I tried to sleep.

But I couldn't. Especially knowing that I'd have to lie there all night, alone, thinking about Autumn at that party, without me.

I found Connor's number crumpled in the pocket of my pants. Midnight had come and gone, but it didn't matter. I flipped open my phone and pounded out a text.

Hey

Then I waited for what seemed like an hour, feeling dizzy and pathetic. Maybe he was at the party. Maybe he'd hold up his phone and show it to everyone. A trophy of my utter humiliation.

My phone vibrated.

Come over

And the next thing I knew, I was sneaking out of my room.

CHAPTER TWENTY

I drove up the long, private road that led to the Hughes Christmas Tree Farm. My headlights flashed across a bunch of cheerful hand-painted signs, nailed to wooden posts and placed every hundred feet along the drainage ditch. VISIT US IN SPRING. HAYRIDES. TRY OUR PUMPKIN BUTTER! They looked weirdly foreboding in the middle of the night.

I ignored the turn for visitors parking, because there was no way I was walking alone in the dark. Instead, I kept driving until I reached the top of his driveway. I killed the engine and cut the lights.

Connor's house sat at the foot of a hill — a huge hunter green Victorian with white wooden shutters on every window and a wraparound front porch. The front door had one of those screens that always slam with a thunderclap. Humongous pumpkins with gnarled stems were set out on every step, along with neatly tied bales of hay. The windows were dark, except for a soft kitchen light casting down on a stove and shiny red tea-kettle. The whole place looked fake, like a house in a painting.

I flipped open my phone to text Connor — and then snapped it shut. Because it occurred to me that Connor might have fallen asleep, even though I'd rushed right over. Or maybe he'd passed out, since he'd obviously been drinking before the dance. A deep embarrassment burned so hot that I opened my window a crack. I would die if Connor saw my text the next morning. He'd know that I'd come here only to drive back home when he hadn't woken up. Those are the kinds of stories people laugh about forever. It would ruin the rest of my senior year. So I came up with a new plan — if I didn't text him, I could say that I was the one who'd decided against coming. That *I* had stood *him* up.

Then I saw him come out from around the side of the house. He'd changed out of his prisoner costume and into a navy hooded sweatshirt, jeans, and a gray wool hat. He walked slowly, confidently. He pulled a hand out of his pocket to wave.

I sucked in a big breath. Okay. This was happening. I was here, he was here, and, in all likelihood, we were going to hook up. As straightforward as that seemed, the moment still felt completely surreal. But I swallowed those feelings down, because I wanted to look relaxed. Like this wasn't a big deal. Because it wasn't. He wasn't. Maybe to some other girls at school, to girls like Spencer, but not to me.

As soon as Spencer crossed my mind, I started thinking about the things she'd said at girls' night. Maybe she did know what she was talking about. I knew what I wanted from Connor tonight. I wanted to forget about Autumn. I wanted company. So long as I wasn't looking for anything more than a distraction, what was wrong with coming here? I wasn't some hopeless romantic, praying that Connor might fall in love with me. In fact, I wanted nothing even close to that. The key was having the power. Using it to get what I wanted. So I got out of the car and casually leaned against my door. I waited for him to come to me.

"Hey," he whispered. "You made it."

"Yeah," I said, and stared off into the dark. "I thought you might be at Bobby's party."

"I was. But I left when I got your text." He smiled and my entire body tensed up. "So . . . do you want to come inside?"

I rolled my eyes. "I'm not going inside. What if your parents wake up?"

He spread his feet apart and rocked his weight from side to side. "They're not going to wake up," he assured me.

I couldn't help but think of all the other girls he'd probably done this with.

I shook my head. "No way."

He glanced in my backseat. "We could hang out in your car."

"Ew. Come on."

"All right, all right," he said, suddenly sounding tired. We were at an impasse. The thing was, I didn't want to go home.

Something in the distance caught his attention. He turned back, excited. "Look, I've got an idea. Stay here."

"Okay . . . ," I said, but it came out like a question. Probably because I had no idea what he had in mind.

He jogged off back to his house, and I was left there, standing alone.

Three mini forests stretched out beyond Connor's house — one to the left, one to the right, and one up the hill. Pine trees were planted in neat rows, like corn. Behind me, there was a gift store made to look like a shed. I saw Christmas ornaments hanging inside, home-made jellies and pantry stuff, and scented candles in tiny mason jars. Planted next to the store was a sizable vegetable garden.

My family had never gotten a Christmas tree from here because they were way too expensive. And after a big long debate on whether we could justify the ecological repercussions of getting a tree, we went to Home Depot, where they set up a little chain-link pen in the parking lot. Those trees were all twenty bucks. Here, you paid for the experience.

Connor came back out of his house. He had a blanket slung over his shoulder and a tin lantern. "Come on, Sterling," he said, and pointed to the woods off to his left. "Let's go for a walk."

I followed him up a narrow path through the evergreen trees. We didn't talk, probably because I stayed a few steps behind him. I couldn't stop looking around. Most of the trees were really tall, but some were the same height as me. I reached out and touched the needles, and they varied as much as the sizes. Sharp, soft, waxy. Little piles of hay had been piled around each tree trunk — to keep them warm, I guessed. It was pretty cold out. I could see my breath. And it was quiet. Freakishly quiet. The night sky was pricked by a million more stars than I could ever see from my house, stars so small they looked like dust.

At the very back edge of the property, we reached a shed with wooden shingles and a pitched roof. It looked like it could be a little kid's playhouse.

Connor fiddled with a padlock, the light from his lantern swishing across the knotted, rough shed walls and brightening the first few fir trees around us.

"We don't use this shed much, except in December," he explained as he jiggled the key. He gave the door a hard tug, but it wouldn't open. Then, when he tried to pull the key out, it got stuck inside the lock. He cursed under his breath.

I waited behind him, hands pushed down deep into the front pockets of my jeans. "It's getting late," I told him, sounding impatient because it was the middle of the night and I was finding it harder with every passing second not to turn around and race back to my car.

Click.

Connor unlatched the padlock and opened the door. The metal hinges squeaked like out-of-tune violin strings. I followed him inside.

The shed smelled like we had climbed up into one of the pine trees — sweet and syrupy green. It was so intense, it made me woozy. I felt my way through the darkness and caught my knee on something. A clatter interrupted the stillness.

Connor held the lantern in my direction. "You okay?" A rack of old metal handsaws appeared next to me, piled high and haphazardly. I'd knocked a few on the floor.

As I assured Connor that I was fine, I reminded myself that we were deep in the woods, so no one would have heard the noise, no one would find us here. But I still felt exposed, vulnerable, with his light trained on me. So I ducked down to the shadows to pick up what had fallen.

Connor hung the lantern from a nail over the door. It cast a dull light on the crowded space. I saw more equipment — bundles of holiday lights, some vintage sleds, a wheelbarrow. He moved some things around, restacking bags of seed and rolls of burlap, and spread the wool blanket down on the small space he'd cleared. He sat down, Indian style, and held out his hand for me.

I hated that I was breathing so hard, panting white clouds of hot breath into the cold air. I knew Connor could tell I was nervous. He didn't know what to do or say. I could see him going over it all in his head. He gave me his number, and I called him and came here. I should know what's next. Except I hesitated, and his hand dropped.

I finally sat next to him, and stretched my legs out. Immediately, they started to quiver, but before he could notice, I leaned in and kissed him fast. I pressed my lips against his, my hair falling around our faces.

He pulled away before I had a chance to open my mouth.

Doubt crept through me. My thoughts shouted inside my head. *Get up, Natalie! Go back to the car!*

Then Connor pushed some the hair out of my face and threaded it behind my ear. His movements were softer and slower than mine. He leaned in close to my face, his eyes dark but glittering, like two lakes in wintertime.

And then he kissed me. This time with lips parted, as if he was whispering into my mouth. I closed my eyes and tried to catch the beat and the rhythm of how this all went. His hands moved up to my shoulders, pulling me closer to him. He was warm — hot, even. I wrapped my arms around his neck, tucked my fingers down into the back of his collar. My whole body folded into his warmth, and then we both lay down. Connor stopped kissing me and grabbed the corners of the blanket, wrapping it around us. We baked inside. It was so hot, and we were moving and pressing and shifting all over each other. My mind completely shut off, and we became the working parts of a motor, circular and precise and perfect.

I was nervous that Connor might try to take things further than I wanted to go, but he didn't.

We only stopped kissing to catch our breath.

This was my least favorite part, when Connor and I were forced to make small talk to fill the awkward pauses.

He asked me seven different times if I wanted some water. I finally said sure, but when I realized that he'd have to go back to the house to get it, I told him to forget it. At some point I asked him if he had any siblings, because it seemed like the kind of basic information you should know about someone you're making out with. I learned he had three older sisters, and forgot their names immediately, although I was pretty sure they all started with the letter C. Connor was the baby. He seemed proud of this, which I found strange.

A very, very small part of me wanted a miracle to happen, where Connor would pull back from my lips and say something profound or beautifully poetic. Because when he touched me, things felt just shy of perfect. Nothing like that happened, though, so instead I let myself enjoy the way he ran his hands through my hair.

I couldn't believe how amazing a simple gesture like that could make me feel, as if my veins were suddenly pumping electricity and not blood.

After a while, the kissing slowed down, and we just lay together, my head on his chest. I hadn't thought about my fight with Autumn since I'd gotten in the car to come here. But I was thinking about her now, wondering if she'd gone home after the party, or if she'd slept over at Marci's house.

I lifted my head and stared down at Connor's sweatshirt, at the Ross Academy football stitched on the center. Being here was like spending the night tucked away in a dream. I was able to forget all my problems for a while. Except I was starting to wake up.

"I'd better get going," I said. I started looking around for my coat.

"Here." He stepped into a dark corner and reappeared with it. It had gotten some sawdust on it, and he brushed it off.

When I took it, I meant to say thank you. But instead I said, "No one can know that I came here to see you. Okay?" He made a strange face, like he didn't understand. "I don't want to be your girlfriend or anything like that." I instantly regretted saying this — not because I didn't mean it, but because it was so presumptuous.

He looked like he was trying to see whether or not I was joking. And then he grabbed me and pulled me close. "You're funny, Sterling." He leaned to kiss me, and I let him, but it was a last kiss, not the start of anything else.

And then I walked to my car by myself, leaving Connor behind to lock up. I left it all behind in the shed. It belonged there. It was not going to be a part of the rest of my life.

CHAPTER TWENTY-ONE

When I woke up around noon, it was as if I'd been dipped in pine sap. Even with my face buried in my pillow, I could still smell the sharply sweet scent. The sheets felt extraordinarily cool and smooth compared with Connor's wool blanket. My body ached from rolling around on the unforgiving wood floor of the shed. But it was a good, secret ache.

That feeling lasted pretty much the whole day, distracting me from my fight with Autumn. I rationed my memories with Connor, taking little sips, just enough to quench my thirst. I had to be careful with what I had until I could get more.

I didn't hear from him for the rest of the weekend, and he didn't hear from me. I had homework and SAT prep. I had to clean my room and my bathroom; I had to get my life in order. It wasn't like I had my cell in my hand, waiting for his call.

If anything, I was waiting for Autumn's.

I figured it was a case of us both needing time to cool down, a little space from each other. I knew we'd work things out soon. After all, we were best friends. We'd never even really gotten into a fight before, not one like this. So I wasn't scared. If anything, it was preparation for what was to come with college. We'd have to get used to spending time apart.

But my mom and dad were suspicious. They kept coming upstairs to check on me, bringing food and drinks and giving me first crack at the Sunday newspaper. I didn't want to talk about my fight with Autumn, but I did invite my mom into my room to watch *Singin' in the Rain* — the next movie on the AFI list. I didn't feel bad about watching it without Autumn, either. It seemed a fitting punishment. And the movie was good, too. Corny and romantic. She would have liked it.

When she hadn't called by Sunday evening, I started to lose my appetite. A few times, I picked up the phone to call her, but I always stopped myself. What would I say? *Did you have fun at the party without me? Are you glad you left me?* I didn't want to ask those questions, because I feared her answers would be yes.

I hardly slept Sunday night, tossed and turned for hours, thinking about what school was going to be like. I even thought about texting Connor to see if he was awake, but talked myself out of that. I didn't want to look desperate. I had to show some restraint.

Monday was the first bitterly cold day of the season, an ominous reminder that winter wasn't far off. The sharp air cut right through my wool tights.

I had no idea what I would do the moment I reached the stop sign at the end of my block. Would I make a left and pick up Autumn, even though we hadn't spoken since the dance? Or would I make a right, and go straight to school? I sat there for a few seconds, staring down to the left at an empty street, until another car came up behind me.

It ended up being a much shorter ride to school without having to cut across town and back for Autumn. Ten minutes, instead of twenty-five. When I stepped out of my car, I shivered. From the cold and the nerves. What would things be like when I saw Autumn? How should I act when I saw Connor? I had no precedent for either situation.

I spent all of homeroom lingering near the door, glancing every so often down the hall at Autumn's locker. I kept imagining her standing in the center of her huge living room window, flanked by her mother's heavy plum drapes, her head turned all the way to the right so she could see down to the stop sign.

I should have picked her up.

But could Autumn really have expected that, after everything that had gone down on Friday, and the silence after? Was I expected to pretend like everything was fine? I couldn't do that. Autumn needed to know that she'd hurt me.

She finally arrived about a minute before the late bell, scampering down the hall to her locker. She had on her red puffer vest and her favorite fuzzy woolen hat, the ivory one with the earflaps that her grandma had knit for her when she'd first started high school. I'd always thought the hat was so goofy, like something a sheep-herding Swedish yodeler would wear. She really liked it, though I hadn't seen her wear it for a couple of years. It wasn't even cold enough for a hat. Not really.

I quickly took my seat, opened my notebook, and pretended to study the calculus equations I'd already memorized over the weekend. But inside, my mind spun numbers and values and x's and y's. I decided that if Autumn did try to talk to me, I'd hear her out, but I wouldn't forgive her. At least not right away.

"Hey!"

I looked up as Autumn walked past me and sat with some other girls in the back of the classroom. A terrible ache swelled in my stomach when I realized that Marci wasn't one of them, and I was quickly running out of people to blame.

CHAPTER TWENTY-TWO

Freshman year, I found a way to get changed out of my bathing suit without ever having to be completely naked. The complicated dance looked anything but graceful, and would certainly give Spencer a huge laugh. But I'd mastered it, and now, as a senior, I could do it faster than any girl in the locker room. Not exactly the kind of talent you'd note on your college applications, but a skill that had served me well.

First, I pulled my arms through my bathing suit straps, and positioned it like a tube top. I wore a navy Speedo one-piece, which fit extra snug. I knew it wouldn't slip down, but I still kept my elbows pinned to my side.

Then I put my bra on over the suit, and as soon as I had it latched, I pulled the suit down to my belly button. That was the trickiest part — moving fast enough to keep the pool water from seeping into the cotton. A second too long and the bra cups would stay damp until well after lunch, which felt as uncomfortable as it sounds.

Next I put on my oxford shirt and did up the buttons, then pulled my skirt up over my hips. After that, I could discreetly trade my bathing suit for my underwear and my spandex shorts, without anyone seeing a thing. Not that any of the other girls were looking.

The bell rang, and I slowly walked up the stairs to the freshman hallway, where Autumn would normally wait for me. I told myself she wouldn't be there. And she wasn't. But Connor was.

He leaned against the big wooden banister, talking to two guys. I could tell he noticed me, the way the corners of his mouth lifted.

I let mine lift, too, and ignored Autumn's braided blond hair bobbing far off down the hallway, already on her way to our next class.

I kept walking. Connor broke off from his friends. He sped up until he was right beside me. But not *with* me. There was just enough vacant space to keep us from looking together.

"You're breaking the rules," I whispered.

"When can I see you again?" he whispered back.

"If you don't get away from me, it'll be never."

But before he could answer, Spencer tackled me.

"Natalie! I've been dying to talk to you all weekend."

"Hey," I said, and watched over Spencer's shoulder as Connor disappeared down the hallway. Then I smiled at her, thinking of my secret. I was sure she'd be proud of the way I was handling Connor.

Spencer looped her arm through mine. "So there's a crazy rumor flying all over school about something shocking that happened this weekend." Her normally high-pitched voice dropped into something deeper, more suspicious and sly.

For a second, I worried that Connor had let something slip. That word had gotten out. And the good feelings I'd had a moment before evaporated. I pulled Spencer over into a corner. "What? What happened?"

"Come on. I'll walk you to class. And along with way, I will tell you the miraculous tale of one girl's takedown of Mike Domski."

The story quickly spilled out: On Sunday, Mike had gotten ahold of Spencer's number. He'd called her and asked if she'd wanted to go to the movies. She had to stop stringing him along, he'd said. The way she'd rubbed against him at the Halloween dance and flirted at Bobby Doyle's party was enough to drive a guy insane.

They had to go on a proper date. Spencer said yes, but she'd told him she had to go to her grandma's house for an early dinner.

"Isn't your grandma dead?" I asked.

Spencer winked.

She told Mike that she would meet him at the theater at eight o'clock.

Mike arrived early. He'd dressed up. He waited outside.

At five minutes until eight, Spencer called Mike and claimed to be stuck in traffic. She asked Mike to go into the theater and save them seats. She didn't want to miss any of the plot, and that way, he could fill her in.

Mike paid for two tickets and left Spencer's with the box office girl. He didn't know what kind of snacks Spencer might like, so he bought a bunch — Twizzlers, popcorn, those little pretzel bits with the cheese inside.

"Wait. I'm actually starting to feel bad for him," I said.

"Remember, this is the guy who defaced your poster, who crashed your girls' night, who —"

"Okay. I'm back. Keep going."

Spencer texted him about ten minutes later. Crawling

traffic, she said, but she was close. And then, something else.

"I told him to whip it out and have it ready for me. He wrote back, *You nasty little girl.*"

"Ew! He did not."

Spencer could barely keep from laughing. "Anyway, a bunch of girls and I were already hiding in the very last row, and we could see him shimmying and wriggling in his seat. I ducked out and found the manager and let him know that there was a boy with his pants down in theater twelve."

"No way!"

"I think the manager wanted to call the police, but when he saw us girls laughing, he just threw Mike out. It was . . . epic. And I think I taught him a lesson for sure."

"How did you know he would do it?"

"Because for the last three weeks, I've been making him think that some kind of dirty hookup was the inevitable end of this ridiculous flirtation we'd been going through."

"I'm proud of you," I told her, which seemed like a weird thing to say, but that was how I felt.

"Okay. I'd better get going. I'll see you later, Natalie."

The bell rang, and I ran to Western Philosophy. Mike Domski came down the hall from the other direction, looking angrier than I'd ever seen him. Jaw set, teeth clenched, gripping the straps of his book bag in two tight fists. I didn't feel bad for him. He deserved to be humiliated. I figured it might even do him some good.

CHAPTER TWENTY-THREE

Connor texted me just after midnight that Friday night. I was surprised and not surprised at the same time.

He was waiting out on the driveway when I pulled up. As soon as I stepped out of the car and into the night, he reached for my hand.

The whole walk up to the shed was a flirtatious build. I started jogging backward, silently daring him to come and get me. Connor made chase, so I turned and sprinted into the woods. He kept pace easily, his hands grabbing at my peacoat. I let him pull it off of me and kept running, managing to stay just out of his reach by circling and dodging around the bristly pines. Both of us were laughing, and we didn't even stop to think someone might hear us. I slipped on a pinecone. Connor caught me in his arms, his hands gripping me through my clothes. He leaned in to kiss me, and when he closed his eyes, I saw my chance and broke free again.

I felt drunk, even though I wasn't. And while I ran away from him, I still raced headlong toward our shed. I couldn't get there fast enough. He came up behind me when I reached the door and fiddled with the lock, his arms wrapped around me, both of us heaving in cold air and blowing out puffs of steam.

He fired up the little lantern, and then we tumbled down to the wool blanket. Connor rolled on his back and brought me on top of him. His hands slipped underneath my shirt. They were cold enough to shock me.

I lifted myself up. "What are you doing?"

"Huh?" Connor's cheeks were red and he was out of breath. "Nothing. Why?"

"Good," I said cautiously, eyeing him as I climbed off his torso and lay next to him on the floor.

He turned on his side and brushed away my hair from my face. Then he started kissing me again. The spot where my neck met my ears, lightly and sweetly, lips barely touching skin.

I closed my eyes and ran my hands through his wavy hair. It seemed odd that I knew how thick it was. But even with that concrete sense, I lost my sense of gravity. I was somewhere between floating and falling — the in-between that feels both scary and awesome.

Connor pulled me on top of him, and his hands slid

up my back again. He watched me. Wide-eyed and grinning like a fool. His fingers tucked underneath my bra strap, then he pinched the closure, trying to pop the hook open.

I rolled off him. "Seriously, Connor."

"What? I'm sorry. Do you not want to?"

"No. I don't want to," I said firmly. "I'm not like that."

Connor's forehead wrinkled. "You're not like *what*?"

I sat up and crossed my legs. "Listen. I might sneak out here to this dirty shed in the middle of the night to spend time with you, but I'm not like the other girls in school. I'm not going to lie back and let you do whatever you want to me. Things are going to go at my pace, or they're not going to go at all. Got it?" I'd hoped to avoid this kind of talk. I'd thought he might be able to read me, and we could have fun with each other and not get all heavy.

Connor started laughing. Really laughing. It was infuriating. "What other girls are you talking about?" he asked.

"Don't play all innocent with me." I second-guessed what I planned to say next, but when Connor didn't look any more serious, I couldn't help myself. "I know you lost your virginity in eighth grade."

"Who told you that?" He sounded pissed, which confused me. First off, boys always bragged about that kind of stuff. And second, everyone knew that Connor had gotten really drunk and had sex with Bridget Roma in her sister's car on New Year's Eve.

I shrugged my shoulders and played it cool. "Lots of people. It's true, isn't it?"

Connor blushed. And not in the shy way. He shook his head, like I'd crossed a line. "I don't know what that has to do with anything. I'm not trying to force you to do anything you don't want to. That's for sure."

"Good." A part of me regretted bringing it up, but I needed to make sure Connor respected me. Now that it seemed settled, I lay back down and tried to pull him close.

Only he turned away from me. "You know what?" he said. "I'm not sure I can shift gears back that fast."

I sat up quickly and was about to say something witty and sharp back when suddenly my left butt cheek burned bad enough for me to gasp.

Connor noticed. "What happened?"

I squinted my eyes in pain. "I think I just got a splinter!"

"Are you kidding?" Connor tried to stifle a laugh.

"Is that hard to believe? Look at where we are,

Connor! Look at this place!" This was my punishment, I figured. "Ack! It really stings."

"Here," Connor said. "Let me see." I rolled over to my knees and stuck my butt up into the air. It was completely humiliating, but what other choice did I have? "You're going to have to take off your jeans."

I could barely swallow. "No way."

"How else am I going to see what's going on down there?" He stood up and grabbed the lantern hanging over our heads.

Ugh, I thought. *So much for boundaries.* I unzipped my pants and pulled my jeans down.

I'd never been undressed in front of a boy before. I knew it would happen eventually. Maybe in a bed-and-breakfast or a nice hotel room. Not a dorm — those were gross. Definitely somewhere nicer than this.

Connor moved the lantern close. I felt its warmth. "Yikes," he said, in a voice serious enough to scare me. "You're bleeding. Just relax. I'm going to lift up your underwear a little bit so I can see. This sucker ripped right through the cotton." His finger slid behind the elastic band and pulled it the tiniest bit down. "Okay. I see it. It's in pretty deep." He fished a red Swiss army knife out of his pocket. My heart raced until I saw he wasn't going for the blade, but the tweezers attachment. "Take a deep breath."

I did — and it was over fast. As soon as the splinter came out, my butt felt slightly better. My ego, not so much. Connor brought the tweezers around to my face to show me the long, brown piece of wood.

"You should probably get home and take care of it. Maybe put some peroxide on it or something, so it doesn't get infected."

"All right." I hadn't exactly envisioned my night ending like this.

Connor walked me back to the car. We didn't hold hands. Instead, I kept a few steps ahead to hide the fact that I was still blushing.

But I did let him kiss me good-bye.

CHAPTER TWENTY-FOUR

I woke up late Monday morning. I'd spent the last three nights in a row with Connor, and the lack of sleep was definitely catching up to me. That, and the fact that it had been ten days since Autumn and I last spoke.

It was yearbook picture day, and I should have gotten right up with the first buzz of my alarm to put some effort into getting ready. After all, my senior portrait wasn't just going to be in the yearbook. I would be immortalized up on the wall in the library, number nine.

Only I kept hitting the snooze button. And when I finally did get out of bed, I barely had enough time to grab a shower.

It wasn't until I'd finished drying off and begun brushing my teeth, that the steam on the mirror dripped away just enough to let me see what had magically appeared overnight.

At first I'd thought it might be a pimple. I touched it lightly with my fingertips hoping to feel a bump, or something to squeeze so it might go down before pictures. But it was a flat, red oval, maybe the size of a quarter, flecked with tiny purple dots of broken capillaries. It sat nearly in the middle of my neck, hovering an inch or so off my collarbone. Where Connor had been kissing me last night.

A hickey. A big fat hickey on my neck for yearbook picture day.

I thought of my senior portrait hanging on the library wall. All those powerful-looking girls, like the young Ms. Bee. Accomplished, serious. And then me, President Hickey. People in the future might assume that I slept my way to being student council president. That splotch sucked all the dignity out of my accomplishment. I'd be remembered forever as a slut.

I ran into my bedroom, before my mom or dad could see me, and slammed the door. I threw on a crisp white oxford and fastened the buttons the way all the girls at school did — leaving three below the collar open. But the hickey shone like a red-bulbed lighthouse from the pale sea of my skin. I tried leaving just two buttons open. Then one. But the only way to completely hide my hickey was to do up every single button. The collar felt like a noose, or one of those stockades in the olden days. Like a punishment I somehow deserved.

Our gymnasium had been turned into a portrait studio. Bright lights stood tall on tripods, catching the dust flying through the air in beams projected on a rich navy velvet curtain. An artsy-looking bald man in tweed slacks stood with his face pressed into the back of his camera.

We'd been called down by grade. A few juniors were left snaking along the court edge, tracing the perimeter of the gym. The flashbulb popped like a pulse. Three, two, one, POP. The photographer shouted, "Next!" The line inched forward. Three, two, one, POP.

Autumn stood across the gym, head cocked to the side as she took out her braids. They left her hair perfectly wavy. Marci Cooperstein stood at Autumn's hip and, along with a bunch of other girls, dug through their makeup bags, suggesting lipsticks and blushes to each other. Marci rubbed a sheer pink lipstick across her lips before handing it to Autumn, who did the same.

I leaned against the gym mats. I didn't have any makeup on, just my trusty Burt's Bees. And my hair was still wet from my shower. I cursed myself for not waking up earlier and getting ready properly. Not to mention the fact that I'd been branded.

Connor came out of the boys' locker room and stood near me, pretending to read the intramurals postings on the bulletin board. "You look nice," he said. "A little buttoned up."

"I have to be!" I hissed. "You gave me a hickey last night. Now my senior portrait is going to be ruined!"

Mike Domski walked by us, and both Connor and I closed our mouths. But as soon as Mike was out of earshot, I laid into Connor again. "Hickeys are absolutely disgusting. It's like . . . when a rancher brands his cattle with one of those hot poker thingies. I don't belong to you. I don't want your mark anywhere on me."

"I'm sorry," he whispered. "I swear I didn't do it on purpose." It sounded like he meant it. But I was so mad I stormed off. That was all I needed on top of everything else: To have someone see us talking, and then notice my hickey and put two and two together.

I ended up two steps behind Mike Domski. I wouldn't have paid attention to a single thing he said, but then he called out, "Hey, Fish Sticks!"

It was pure reflex, the way my gut seized up. I wondered if Marci would defend Autumn the way I used to, though I highly doubted it. Marci cared too much about what guys like Mike Domski thought of her.

Only Marci didn't even need to defend Autumn.

Autumn spun around, smiled, and said, "Hey, Domski."

I couldn't believe it. Not only had Autumn forgiven Marci, but now she was actually answering to *Fish Sticks*? I glared at her. But either she pretended not to notice me, or she really didn't.

One of the photographer's assistants clapped her hands and herded us over to the bleachers. "We're going to need everyone in the designated senior picture attire." She pulled a fistful of fabric strips from inside her apron pocket. "Ties and blazers are mandatory for the boys, so if you don't already have both on, come see me." She stepped behind a curtain and dragged a big cardboard box over to us. "And I've got black smocks for the girls. Please slide them on and make sure your bra straps aren't visible."

I stepped over to the box and picked up one of the smocks. I'd completely forgotten that this was what the senior girls wore for yearbook portraits. It was like a poncho, a deep V-neck sweater that slid over our heads. Other girls around me draped them on and then unbuttoned their shirts. It left your shoulders and your neck bare.

I jogged over to the assistant. "Excuse me. I wanted to see if I could take my portrait in my uniform."

She looked at me queerly. "Are you a senior?"

"Yes."

"Then I'm afraid that's not possible."

"But this is the uniform I've worn for four years. It has . . . sentimental value! Plus, the boys essentially get to wear their uniforms. If I can't wear mine, that amounts to sexism."

I tried to sound serious, but the photography assistant laughed at me. And suddenly the reality of the situation squeezed my chest and made it impossible to breathe. While everyone else got into line, I grabbed my smock and sprinted to the bathroom.

I'd stolen some foundation from my mother's vanity before leaving the house. Now I tipped my finger in the bottle and covered my fingertip in the thick, velvety liquid. Then I tried to dot some makeup along the lighter edges of the hickey, blending it into the thick center. My hands shook, I was so upset. Unfortunately, my mom's skin was a couple shades darker than mine, thanks to my Sicilian grammy. The purple oval bled out into a haze of sickly orange. Instead of covering up the hickey, it only attracted more attention to it. The tears started coming.

I heard the door open. Spencer came in. "Hey, Natalie!" she said, oblivious, walking over to the sink.

"Ugh. I dissected a frog last period and though I've washed my hands a hundred times, they still smell like formaldehyde." She turned to look at me, and I felt her eyes narrow on my neck. "Whoa! Who'd you get *that* from?"

"It's a bug bite," I said, flatly. I didn't have time for this.

"Right. A bug bite. In November." She dug inside her bag. "That happens *all the time*."

I could feel Spencer lording it over my head. She knew exactly what was on my neck. She stepped forward with a wet paper towel and tucked her makeup case under her arm. "Here. Wipe that stuff off."

I stared down at the paper towel as it dripped a puddle on the floor. "I'm fine," I said. "Thanks."

"Natalie, quit being so proud and let me help you. Unless you want a big hickey dead center in your senior portrait." She pushed some hair off my shoulder for a better look. "So who's the lucky guy?"

I took the paper towel and rubbed it hard and fast against my neck. "Look — this is a bug bite, okay? If you want to help me, great. If you don't, well, then get out of here."

Spencer seemed like she wanted to say something,

but she held it in and instead tilted my head back gently. Then she pulled the cap off a bright yellow crayon.

"What's that?" I said.

"The yellow makes your skin appear less red. I'll put this on first, then a layer of foundation, and then . . ." She dug in her makeup bag. "I'll put some powder on top. You and I are almost the same shade."

Three minutes later, I was transformed into a good girl. Spencer dabbed a last bit of powder on my neck. "There. Your, uh, bug bite has vanished." She also gave me some lipstick and put my head under the hand dryer while she raked her fingers through my damp hair. I came out of the whole thing looking halfway decent.

"Make sure you pose with your chin tilted down a little," she instructed, pulling some of my hair over my shoulder. "Don't worry. You look really pretty, Natalie."

"Thanks," I said. And I was thankful, even though I couldn't look at her. The girl I used to babysit had just saved my ass big time.

I went back into the gym with my smock on and my white shirt balled in my hand. Ms. Bee stood off to the side with another teacher, watching. I walked past her, and made sure that my chin was down, like Spencer had said.

Out of the corner of my eye, I saw Connor staring at me.

Three, two, one, POP.

CHAPTER TWENTY-FIVE

We kept seeing each other. Not just weekends, but school nights, too. In secret. In the shed.

Fifth time. Sixth time. Seventh.

The eighth time, Connor pushed the door open and handed me the lantern. For whatever reason, he wanted me to walk in first.

The itchy stadium blanket was folded in half on the floor. Unfurled on top was a puffy sleeping bag, unzipped enough to reveal a plaid fleece lining. A pillow leaned against a cardboard box as if it were a head-board, in a pillowcase with edges trimmed in white eyelet lace.

"Is this your mom's?" I asked uneasily, lifting it up off the floor. It had already gotten a little dirty. I brushed away what I could.

"She's got an entire closetful. She won't notice." Connor hung my peacoat on a nail. Then he pulled out a couple of tea light candles from the pouch of his sweat-shirt, lit them, and set them on top of a rafter. Flickering light lit up the peaks and corners of the shed like a cathedral. "I thought we could use a warmer bed, since it's getting pretty cold out here." It was true. The last couple times, I'd been so freezing I'd lost feeling in my toes. "It's the best solution I could come up with, since you still refuse to come inside my house. . . ." He let his words hang in the air, as if I might change my mind.

I looked down. Connor had even swept the floor. There were no pine needles, no sawdust. "You didn't have to go to all this trouble," I mumbled. I appreciated the effort, of course. But I was already too comfortable in this shed, considering the circumstances. This was not a romantic cottage in the woods, and Connor Hughes was not my boyfriend. I had to keep everything in perspective or I would lose perspective entirely.

"You're welcome." Connor smiled, then lifted his sweatshirt. His T-shirt went up with it, and he tossed them both into an empty red wheelbarrow.

I tried not to stare. His abs were carved and defined, rippling down to the waistband of his nylon track pants. Which he also proceeded to slip off, leaving him in a pair of striped boxers and white socks pulled up to his calves. The smell of soap on his skin was intense.

"Call me crazy," I said, "but you might stay warmer if you kept your clothes on."

Connor laughed. "Are you kidding? This sleeping bag is rated for ten degrees below zero. I used it when my dad and I went ice fishing last winter. If you and I don't take our clothes off, we'll sweat to death." Suddenly all the layers I'd cleverly thought to put on to fight the cold — a pair of thermal underwear, jeans, two pairs of socks, sweatshirt, T-shirt, and a cami — felt suffocating. He slid into the sleeping bag. "C'mere, Sterling."

I stared down at his grinning face. "I don't think I'll fit."

"It's plenty big enough for two." He shimmied over and patted the empty space next to him, a sliver of room.

The wind outside leaked between the cedar shingles and sent the candles flickering. It hit me that, fancy sleeping bag or not, Connor and I couldn't meet out here much longer. It would be way too cold. And though the farm was quiet now, come holiday time there'd be workers in and out of here for supplies, and customers meandering all over our private maze of pines, on the hunt for the perfect Christmas tree. Part of me felt relieved at this very clear expiration date. But I felt sad, too. I had always looked forward to winter, to mittens and colored lights, hot chocolate and velvet bows, corny Christmas songs and the search to find the best present possible for Autumn. The probability of us not exchanging gifts this year felt more real than I wanted it to.

I took off my first layer of clothes — the jeans and my sweatshirt — and hung them up with my peacoat. It took some work to get comfortable next to Connor. We were squished so tightly together that our foreheads and the tips of our noses touched. It was too close to look at each other without getting a headache, so we both closed our eyes.

It only took a minute for my body temperature to roar. A drop of sweat rolled down the side of my face.

"Here," he said, and lifted off my thermal. The cami underneath went along with it. I probably would have been more self-conscious, except that I still had the thermal leggings and my bra on, and with the sleeping bag, he couldn't really see anything. In fact, I had yet to be completely undressed in front of Connor. His hands had touched nearly all of me, but his eyes hadn't seen a thing. Even though I was sticky from sweat, Connor didn't seem to mind. We kissed for a bit, and his hands ran lightly over my back.

"What do you do when you're not here with me?" he asked.

"I sleep," I said with a smile.

"No. I mean, seriously."

His questions made me anxious. I definitely didn't have a social life like Connor's. "Well, I'm usually with Autumn." My mind searched for other things to tell him, but I drew a blank. A pathetic blank.

"She's a nice girl. I've seen her out a few times lately. How come you don't go to parties with her?"

I rolled over, and then back again, trying to get comfortable. "Of course she's a nice girl. Why wouldn't she be a nice girl?" I knew Autumn wanted to be more social, but I hadn't known she was completely back in the scene.

"I . . . I didn't mean anything by it."

"Just so you know, the things that Chad Rivington said about her weren't true." I wrestled to get my arms out from underneath me. "And to answer your question, Autumn and I don't go to parties together because we're in a fight right now." I wanted add, *That's why I come here to see you*, but I didn't. It wasn't Connor who I was angry with. It was Autumn. And a little bit me, too.

"Over what?"

The sleeping bag had become a microwave. "Can you unzip this thing? I'm suffocating."

Connor fumbled to get his arm across me. The zipper purled open, and it felt like coming up for a breath after a long underwater swim.

"Sorry. I didn't mean to —"

"It's fine. I'm just better off if I don't really think about it."

"Okay. I'll change the subject. You doing anything this Friday?"

I narrowed my eyes. Was he joking? "No. The SATs are Saturday morning."

Connor shrugged.

"Wait," I said. "You're not taking them?"

"Nah."

"But what about college?"

"I'm not going to college." Connor must have seen the surprise on my face, because he started shaking his head, like I had the wrong idea. "Wait — that's not exactly true. I'm going to take a couple of business classes at the community college. But the family business is shifting over to me in the next year or two, when my dad retires."

I said, "That's cool," though I doubt I sounded convinced. Taking over a business like the Hughes Christmas Tree Farm was impressive, but that would mean staying in Liberty River for the rest of your life. Which, to me, seemed like the worst thing possible.

I tried to think of a graceful way to change the subject when Connor started kissing me again. It was like neither of us wanted to admit how different we were, deep down.

So we didn't. Instead, we slithered all over each other, like two snakes in a bag.

A while later, Connor got up to get me a bottle of water from a stash he'd set on a shelf. When he got back in the sleeping bag, his skin was icy. He rubbed next to me to get warm and said, "I like hanging out with you." He rolled on his back and stared up at the ceiling, as if he could see stars and not a bunch of seed bags suspended in between the rafters. When I didn't say anything, Connor pulled me on top of him. "Do you like coming here?"

"I wouldn't be here if I didn't," I said.

It wasn't exactly a declaration of feelings, but it was all I could give him.

CHAPTER TWENTY-SIX

On the drive home that night, I decided that it was time Autumn and I talked. I'd given her space, maybe too much. The trick was getting to her when Marci wasn't around.

Autumn must have felt the same way, because on Friday after school, I found her outside the library, a pile of books in her hands, one knee perched up against the wall. I knew she was waiting to see me, because for the first time since the Halloween dance, she actually made eye contact. I was no longer invisible, the ghost of a friend she used to have.

"Hey," she said. "Can we talk?"

I looked at my watch. The student council meeting would start in five minutes. As much as I wanted this to happen, there were too many students passing us on the way into the library. And I didn't want to feel rushed. We had a lot to discuss.

"Can this wait until after the meeting?" I asked. "I could drive you home. Or we could go somewhere and get food." My mind raced with the possibility. We'd grab dinner at our favorite diner, finally hash things out, and then head back to my house. I still had the *Singin' in the Rain* DVD I'd spitefully watched with my mom after our fight. I'd pretend that I hadn't watched it. That I'd waited for her.

She shook her head. "This won't take long."

The floor went out beneath me. I couldn't believe her. She'd finally decided it was time for us to talk, and I was expected to drop everything? Now I definitely didn't want to get into it before the meeting started, because I could already feel the tightness in my throat.

"I don't know what you suddenly need to tell me," I said. "You've made it clear that you don't want to be friends anymore." I tried to keep my voice down, but it felt like I was screaming.

"I'm quitting student council." Her hand went up to her mouth to bite her fingernail, but she quickly pulled it back down.

I shook my head. "What? Why would you do something like that? Do you honestly hate me that much? God, has Marci completely brainwashed you against me?"

"This isn't about you, or Marci, or anyone. I just don't want to be in student council anymore."

"What about all the committees you volunteered for? You're just going to walk out on your responsibilities?"

"It's not fair to everyone that I haven't been giving it my all." She sounded like it was a pain to have to explain herself. "And quit acting so shocked, Natalie. You knew I was never really into student council."

"Maybe not, but you always had good ideas. Like asking Connor for the bonfire wood and holding our own girls' night. And it's not like student council was bad for you. How's it going to look on your college applications if you quit during senior year?" I threw my hands up. "I really don't get this, Autumn. It's like you're having a midlife crisis or something. I don't want you to do something you're going to regret later on."

"I don't want regrets, either. That's why I want to spend my senior year doing other things. I've missed out on a ton. I've got to make up for lost time before high school is over."

So three years of our friendship was *lost time*? Over Autumn's shoulder, I caught sight of someone poking her head around the corner, watching us. Marci Cooperstein. It was the final straw. "Wow," I said. "Okay. I never thought you'd be stupid enough to make such a terrible mistake again, but apparently I was wrong about you."

Autumn didn't back down. "I'm not making a mistake. And don't you dare judge me."

I couldn't help but laugh. "Judge you? I was the only one in this entire school who *didn't* judge you! You think it was easy for me to be your friend? To always have to protect you? It wasn't. It sucked, actually."

Autumn looked genuinely pissed now. "Don't make it seem like you were some kind of saint. No one wanted to be friends with you. Nobody even liked you! You walked around this school with your nose stuck up in the air, so much smarter, so much better than everyone else. Without me, you wouldn't have had one single friend. No wonder you wanted me to feel so bad about myself. If I hadn't, we would have stopped being friends a long time ago."

I am a good friend, I thought. *A good friend who didn't deserve to be treated this way.* Yes, I'd always been worried about Autumn leaving me. But I'd never made her feel bad about herself in order to make her stay.

I turned to walk away, because really I'd had enough, but then I spun back around. The words were hot in my mouth and I spit them like fireballs:

"You realize you're making a humungous fool out of yourself, don't you, *Fish Sticks*?"

I wanted Autumn to get mad, as mad as I felt. But

instead of turning bright red, all the color drained from her face.

"I never, ever thought you would say that to me," she said.

Black smoke bloomed inside me. I knew I should shut up; I wanted to suck the words back inside my mouth, but I couldn't. I couldn't stop. "But that's your name, right? That's what your *friend* Mike Domski calls you."

"I felt bad for Mike after what Spencer did to him. She humiliated him in front of everyone."

"Are you kidding me? Mike made both of our lives miserable, and now you're sticking up for him? Come on, Autumn! Don't you have any self-respect?"

"I probably should have expected this from you. After all, you're the one who makes me feel the worst about myself! You constantly bring up the whole Fish Sticks thing. How I should tell other girls about it, so they can learn from my mistakes. How I shouldn't be friends with anyone but you, because other people laughed at me. Well, I'm tired of it!" She was releasing her own fire and smoke now. "So people said shitty things about me. You know what? I gave them too much power. I should have never let something so ridiculous affect me the way it did. Especially when it wasn't even true!"

Her words burned so bright, I couldn't see. I couldn't say anything in my own defense. All I could do was cry.

I half-thought Autumn might reach out for me. Or at least apologize, when she saw how badly she was hurting me. After all, I'd held her through so many sobbing fits. I'd dried her tears a thousand times.

But she stayed on her side of the invisible divide, and wiped her cheeks, which were slick with tears, too.

"You've been a great friend to me, Natalie. I'm not saying you haven't. But I don't need you to protect me anymore. I don't need you making me feel bad, or reminding me of something stupid I did three years ago. I'm moving on with my life. And you should, too."

She said it like it would be easy, and maybe for her it was. But for me, crying alone in the hallway, it seemed utterly impossible.

CHAPTER TWENTY-SEVEN

I set myself on autopilot. Some unknown force took over my controls, while I curled up in a ball deep in the back of myself. It dried my tears and pulled me together. It walked me into the library, sat me down at the head of the table, and led an entire student council meeting, filling four of my notebook pages with action items and project discussions and thoughts for next week's agenda. Then it drove home, ate the ziti my mom had cooked, and pushed me up the stairs to my room.

I still couldn't believe that I'd called Autumn *Fish Sticks*. The words left a dirty taste in my mouth even now. Any chance we might have had to patch things up, I had completely ruined. I ached to take it back. But I knew that I couldn't.

My phone buzzed from the bottom of my book bag. I checked and saw who it was, but I couldn't answer. I couldn't go to him. Not tonight.

The SATs were hours away, the most important test of my life. I couldn't screw that up, no matter what kind of shambles my life was in. I shook thoughts of Connor out of my head and stayed focused. I spent an hour reviewing my vocab lists, looked over my essay bullet points, and packed my bag with test-taking essentials — two protein bars, a bunch of my favorite mechanical pencils, a hair tie. And then I tried to sleep. Sleep would be good for me.

But I tossed and turned for what seemed like hours. Sometime in the last two weeks I'd become nocturnal. My body burned energy I didn't know I was even capable of storing up. Even when I lay as still as I possibly could, all my organs and muscles churned like a locomotive. It was anxiety, it was apprehension, it was grief. I tried watching television. I tried reading a book. I tried taking a shower with the water as hot as I could stand.

When I stepped out, I caught a blur of myself in the steamed-up mirror. I looked like a ghost, and felt like one, too. Using my towel's edge, I wiped away the condensation.

Almost instantly, negative things jumped out. I wished that I had bigger boobs; mine were barely a handful. I turned sideways and stared at the dimpled skin on my upper thigh. The scars looked like I'd sat on gravel, from where Grammy's dog had bitten me. I twisted to see the dirt-smudge birthmark on my hip and back again to see my outie belly button, which protruded so far off my stomach that it looked like a third nipple.

I thought: *Is this the kind of stuff Connor would see if I let him look at me naked?*

I knew he liked my body in the dark. His hands were always moving, always touching. And he'd press against me so hard, like he was afraid I'd disappear if given the space to breathe.

The light in my bathroom was harsh, and I felt I deserved that. I despised the girl staring back at me. This was the girl Autumn hated. This was the girl no one really liked. I couldn't stand looking at her. So I shut off the bathroom light and lit a candle that I kept by the sink.

Everything got softer. The ripples on my thigh disappeared. I uncoiled the towel from my head and let my hair fall down onto my shoulders in cold clumps. I leaned forward, putting my hands on the sink edge. More shadows, more curves appeared.

I didn't look like myself. I looked . . . hungry. Starved for affection, for someone who'd make me feel good about myself. I looked like I knew what I was doing when I very clearly did not. Because I didn't understand how being with Connor could feel so right one moment and so pointless the next. Not that it mattered. I was living life in moments, in darkness, in that shed.

I wrapped myself back up in the towel, blew out the candle, and tiptoed across the hall into my room. My phone was buzzing again. Connor, surely. Not Autumn. Never again Autumn. I grabbed it, planning to text him back that I wasn't coming over tonight. Because, really, this whole thing was stupid and bound to blow up in my face. There was really no other way it could end.

He wrote:

Please?

One word, and I was gone.

CHAPTER TWENTY-EIGHT

The idea of me showing up late to the SATs would have been laughable a few weeks before, along with the notion that Autumn and I would no longer be friends, or that I'd spend my nights in the woods. But that was my life. So maybe I shouldn't have been so shocked after all.

I got to school with mere seconds to spare. Ms. Bee, the proctor for my room, stood at the open classroom door, frowning down at her wristwatch. When she looked up and saw me racing down the hall as fast as my legs would carry me, her face was a blend of relief and disappointment. I'd seen her look angry before, but never straight on. Only from the sides, the periphery, aimed at someone else. I thought of about a million excuses in the span of a second, but when I opened my mouth, she shook her head and pointed inside. "No time, Natalie. We've got to get started."

The last open seat in the classroom happened to be directly behind my now-former best friend.

If Autumn was at all concerned that I wouldn't have arrived on time, she didn't look it. As soon as I came in the room, she leaned over and started to root around in her bag, avoiding my eyes. It was a big slap in the face, considering Autumn probably wouldn't have taken a single SAT prep course if it hadn't been for me. I was practically her private tutor, passing on the knowledge I'd gotten from my summer course and all the manuals I'd read. Did she think about that? Did she remember how much I'd done to prepare her for today? I walked past her without crying or saying anything, but inside I wondered if I could really do this for a whole year. If we could reinvent ourselves as strangers.

Ms. Bee handed out the test booklets. I stared at my future, a page full of empty circles. I'd worked way too hard for way too long to prepare for this day. I needed to push everything out of my head and get serious. This, ultimately, was my ticket to escape Liberty River, this life that I'd suddenly screwed up.

Except when the test started, I ignored my booklet and stared at the back of Autumn's head, boring holes into her skull, trying to think about what could possibly be going on in her mind.

And the truth was, I felt tired. I'd been all over Connor last night, kissing him so hard I'd barely breathed. Plus, the heat was on high in the classroom, the dry and hissing heat that was perfect for naps.

I don't remember falling asleep. Just the earthquake that woke me.

I looked up. Everyone in the room did. Ms. Bee used my desk for balance. She had one high heel off, bending over slightly to examine her big toe. She'd bumped my desk leg so hard that my pencil had fallen and rolled halfway across the classroom floor. I wiped away the wetness on my cheek, but there was nothing I could do about the translucent stain of drool right smack in the center of my test booklet.

"Excuse me," Ms. Bee announced, as if it had been an accident. The look she gave me before returning to the front of the room was one of unmistakable, purposeful disappointment.

I recovered and finished as much of the test as I could.

But I still felt like an absolute failure.

CHAPTER TWENTY-NINE

Somewhere in the middle of our make-out session that night, Connor stopped kissing me and started thinking. Which was exactly what I had been trying to avoid.

"What are you doing?" I asked, when he pulled away mid-kiss.

"I can tell you're upset."

"No I'm not."

"I'm not dumb, Sterling." Connor rolled off me and onto his back. "What's wrong?"

It was a straightforward question, but the answers in my brain were a knotted mess I didn't want to untangle. I flipped onto my stomach and pressed my face into the pillow. "Connor. Please. I don't want to get into it right now."

"Then go ahead and change the subject. But I'm not messing around with you when you're like this."

"Why not? I thought guys like you were always good to go."

"It's making me feel gross."

I lifted my head and glared at him. "Thanks a lot."

"You know what I mean."

"All right, fine. I've got a question for you." I smiled a very sweet, very fake smile. "Who did you vote for? For student council president?"

Connor suddenly looked uneasy. "Isn't that an invasion of voter privacy or something?"

"So it *was* Mike." I tugged hard on the blanket to give me a little extra — Connor was a blanket hog. "Figures."

"Mike's my friend. Of course I voted for him." He said it like I should have known that already. Like there was no possible way he would have voted for me.

I turned away from him. I didn't know why it stung so much. Maybe because, deep down, I'd hoped that Connor secretly *had* voted for me. Which was stupid.

Connor curled his body against mine. "I think you're doing a really good job as president, if that counts for something. I'd vote for you now."

I knew why. I knew all Connor's reasons. "It doesn't, but thanks anyway."

"Really? That doesn't make it better? Not even a little?"

I stared hard into the dark, mad at myself for bringing this up in the first place. "No. It makes it worse."

"Look, Sterling. I didn't know you then."

"I hate to break it to you, Connor, but you still don't."

He let out a deep, exasperated sigh. I felt it against my back. "You're not exactly an expert on me, either. You still haven't come to any of my football games. Even though I'd like it if you did."

"I despise football, not to mention all the guys on your team."

"I know you have your issues with my friends. Especially Mike, and I can't blame you for that. When I saw how he screwed up your campaign poster, I got so pissed I took it down myself."

I blushed. "You did that?"

"Come on. I've got sisters, and if a guy ever wrote stuff like that about them, I'd lose my mind. Mike doesn't think sometimes. He doesn't have the best judgment." Connor sat up. "But I'm not Mike. You know that, right?"

"Maybe." I wanted to believe that Connor was smarter, sweeter than I'd originally thought. But I couldn't completely ignore the truth, either. Connor had some very questionable friends, not to mention a long history of girls he'd fooled around with. I had to be careful, even if I didn't exactly want to be.

Connor took the tip of my ponytail and drew a circle in the palm of his hand, as if it were a paintbrush. "I may not know you, but I'm trying. I want to figure you out."

My throat got tight. "Maybe you shouldn't."

"Why?"

"Because that's not what this is supposed to be."

As soon as I said it, I worried what Connor would say. Would he confirm my deepest fears, that our relationship was purely physical? Or would he tell me he had real feelings for me?

Both prospects scared me.

Luckily, Connor didn't say anything. Quite possibly because he was as confused as me. And in a strange way, that was comforting.

I took advantage of his silence and stood up. "I should probably go," I announced. I scanned the floor for my socks, tiptoeing through the darkness on a freezing cold floor.

I heard him get up. And then I felt myself be spun around. Connor wrapped his arms around me tight.

That's when I realized that we'd never offically

hugged before. We'd touched so many different parts of each other, independent pieces that made up the whole of us, but never something so all encompassing. Even though I felt the urge to push him away, I didn't. I just let Connor hold me. And I might even have held him back.

CHAPTER THIRTY

"I notice you've been . . . distracted."

I shifted in my seat and stared at the pointed toes of Ms. Bee's high heels. It was the Monday after the SATs, and if she'd wanted to fail me a thousand times over, I probably would have agreed to it. I felt *that* guilty.

"I know," I said. "I'm sorry."

"Natalie, I know you've been working hard, and you've got a lot on your plate. But your recent behavior concerns me. Thanksgiving is this week, and we're completely unprepared to assemble the food baskets. We need to begin making announcements for the students to bring food donations, get in touch with the local shelter, see how many families are —"

Clearly I needed to cut back the time I spent with Connor. And the time I thought about him. Because I was thinking about him far too much.

"Natalie? Are you even listening?" She put her teacup

down on her desk so hard, a few drops of brown liquid sloshed past the lip.

"Yes. Of course."

Ms. Bee narrowed her eyes. She was not amused. "I've already finished a draft of your college recommendation letter. Please don't compel me to revise it."

That caught me completely off guard. Would Ms. Bee really do something like that? Was the good reputation I'd worked so hard to make for myself in jeopardy? I nodded, apologized profusely, grabbed my coat, and got out of there as quickly as possible.

That's the thing with secrets — you can't explain yourself. The only thing you're left able to say is *sorry* — again and again.

I had just turned on my car when Spencer knocked on the window, her arms wrapped around herself. She wasn't wearing a coat, even though there were hardly any leaves left on the tree branches.

"Hey, Natalie. Do you think I could get a ride home? My mom got stuck at work, and the next bus won't come for at least an hour."

"Sure," I said, and leaned over to click my passenger-side door open. The gesture sparked a sad sensory memory. It felt like forever since I'd done that for someone.

"Thanks!" Spencer settled into the seat and slammed the door. Her teeth were chattering, and she started rubbing her bare legs. I cranked up the heat and pointed all the vents at her. "I owe you big-time," she said.

After Ms. Bee's lecture, I wasn't really in the mood to talk. Luckily, Spencer was in a chatty mood, and she gossiped about a bunch of people in between giving me directions to her apartment building. I didn't have to say much.

And then, peering at my neck, Spencer teased, "So . . . have you gotten any more bug bites lately?"

It was weird. Instead of being defensive, I thought about telling Spencer everything. And I would have, if it wasn't Connor I was kissing. First of all, Spencer had liked Connor. She'd worn his name on her Rosstitute shirt. I didn't think she still had feelings for him, but I wasn't positive. Plus, I didn't exactly trust Spencer's discretion. All she'd need to do was tell one person, and the secret would be out. I'd look like the biggest hypocrite in the world. Which I guess I kind of was.

But then I remembered what Autumn had said to me in the hallway. She'd moved on, made new friends. Why was I so intent on keeping Spencer at arm's length? She'd proven herself to me more than a few times. And whether I liked it or not, Spencer understood boys in a way that I didn't.

"All right. I *am* seeing someone," I said, casually. And then quickly added, "He's not from around here."

If not for her seat belt, Spencer might have popped straight out of her seat. "I knew it! Oh, my God, tell me everything about him! Is he cute? I bet he is so cute."

I turned to her and smiled. So many adjectives filled my mouth. But I could see Spencer's apartment building looming ahead. I didn't want to drop her off. It felt so good to have a girlfriend. Why hadn't I done this weeks ago? So when I braked for a stop sign, I turned to her and asked, "Do you maybe want to go grab a bite to eat? My treat."

Spencer grinned from ear to ear. She looked grateful, as if she were lucky to receive such an invitation from me.

I drove us to what used to be Autumn and my favorite diner, which was an old-timey steel trailer with a handful of tables and a bright-pink neon sign. The place was pretty empty since it was still a few hours from dinnertime. Our waitress let us have our pick of seats, and Spencer opted for the last booth on the right. We had a view of the parking lot and our own push-button juke-box stocked with oldies. Spencer dug for quarters to give us a soundtrack.

We each ordered a Coke and a crock of onion soup baked over with a bubbling cheese canopy, and we shared a plate of perfectly crispy fries drowning in gravy. I was so incredibly happy.

Spencer gladly let me yammer on and on about a slightly altered version of Connor. I kept lots of the details the same. How handsome he was, how he was attracted to the fact that I was such a smart and strong girl. The only thing I changed were the details on how we'd met — my new boyfriend had been my tutor in an SAT prep class, a brilliant college freshman.

"So, what's the issue?" Spencer asked. "He sounds great."

Hearing her say that made my heart hurt. Connor and I were so close to perfect, but still so far.

"We're just . . . very different people," I said.

"And?"

"And nothing. I don't see us having a future. We're like . . . wasting each other's time."

Spencer's face wrinkled. "What do you mean, future? You're not going to be one of those girls who gets married at eighteen, are you?"

"What?" I said, grabbing another napkin. "No! Of course not."

"Well, then, what kind of future are you talking about?"

I thought of our cold little shed. "He's transferring to another college after Christmas. And I don't want to get attached."

Spencer dabbed her fry into a pool of ketchup. "You won't get attached," she said, matter-of-factly.

"I won't?"

"No. Because you already know you can't. It's mind over matter, Natalie. You can't get attached, so don't get attached. It's as easy as that."

"Oh."

"Get what you can out of it. I mean, if spending time with him makes you happy, do it. Don't overthink things. Remember, you've got the power. He wants to be with you. You're the one in charge."

Somehow I managed to nod. Spencer clearly had her sexuality in check. She could turn it off or on, depending on what, or who, she wanted. But I was the complete opposite. I didn't feel like the one in charge. Though it wasn't like Connor was in charge, either. The recklessness was leading both of us.

"Don't get quiet on me now, Natalie. I want details!"

"Like what?"

"You know!" Spencer wiggled her pinky at me.

"What does that mean?"

"Haven't you seen all the girls do this in the hall-way?" She wiggled her pinky again, but I was still clueless. "I invented a hand gesture for Mike Domski. It means *teeny peeny*, and it's caught on like wildfire."

I winced. "Oh, God!"

"Yeah, I know. I've always had my suspicions, and my movie theater prank proved I was right. It's sad, but makes total sense if you think about it. I mean, Mike drives the biggest SUV in the school parking lot!" She laughed a little and then pointed to her lap. "So your guy is all good down there?"

I fidgeted in my seat. "Yeah. I mean, I don't know. It's normal, I guess."

"Well, is he good in bed?"

"What?!"

Spencer pursed her lips. "Don't be coy with me. I'm not a little kid anymore."

"Spencer, I'm not sleeping with him." She stared me down, as if I were lying. "I'm a virgin." And then I looked around for our waitress. After all, we weren't even eating anymore. Just talking.

Spencer looked confused. "Like a total sex virgin? Or

240

a straight-up intercourse virgin? Because I haven't had complete sex with anyone before, either, though I've done *lots* of other stuff."

I grabbed my soda glass. It was empty, but I still sucked down a big gulp of melted ice because I didn't want to talk about this anymore. Because I was picturing Spencer in her Rosstitute shirt, and then in her Halloween costume, and whatever she had to do to convince Mike Domski to whip it out in a movie theater. And I didn't want to be that kind of girl.

I switched the subject to student council, and how much pressure I was under with the Thanksgiving food baskets. The stress gripped me tighter. Spencer listened to every word as intently as the sex stuff, which was somewhat of a relief.

After we finished our food, I drove Spencer back home. "I'm here for you, Natalie," she said as I pulled up in front of her building. "If you need extra help with the baskets, or if you just want to talk, let me know."

I said, "Thanks," only because I would need her help with the baskets. But Spencer and I weren't going to have another conversation like this again. Part of me thought Spencer was a smart girl. And the other part of me thought she was a fourteen-year-old Rosstitute who knew even less than I did.

CHAPTER THIRTY-ONE

That night, we were only a few feet away from the shed before I pivoted and started walking in the opposite direction.

I didn't know why. It wasn't like I had all the time in the world. My parents had gone to bed late, which kept me from sneaking out at a respectable hour. And I couldn't stay long, not with the huge trig test the next morning that I'd hardly studied for. I needed a decent night's sleep. I'd told Connor exactly that on the phone. I had maybe an hour tops. It might not even be worth it.

He'd said to come anyway.

So I did.

And even though he knew tonight would be rushed, Connor didn't say anything about it, about me not going right to the shed.

The first time I came to the farm at night, everything seemed pretty spooky — the darkness, strange noises from the woods. But I felt comfortable here now. I walked around like it was daytime. My eyes took almost no time to adjust to the night once my headlights clicked off.

The gift shop sat a few feet in front of me, so I headed that way. I'd always wanted a closer look at it.

"Mom had it built two years ago. She thought we should sell souvenirs. In fact, it was her idea that we open the farm year-round, instead of just at Christmas. She's got a real business mind." Connor slouched against a porch post. "You'd like her," he added.

Hearing that made me happy. But only for a second, because I wasn't sure Mrs. Hughes would like me back. Not if she knew how many nights I'd sneaked onto her property to fool around with her son while she and her husband were sleeping. No mother in her right mind would like that kind of girl. That was the worst part of all, really: knowing better, but doing it anyway, no matter how deeply it went against the kind of person I was.

I cupped my hands around my eyes to peer through a window at a stack of shelves. Mason jars sat in perfect rows. Handwritten labels proclaimed strawberry jam, apple butter, and pumpkin pie filling in charmingly perfect penmanship. Each one had a scrap of fabric tied over the lid with a piece of twine. Red gingham, like summertime picnic tablecloths.

"She makes everything herself, with fresh ingredients from her garden. Some fancy bakery in the city even started selling her stuff." Connor leaned into me from behind, his body blocking me from the night chill. He rested his chin on my shoulder and looked inside, too. Together, our breath fogged the glass. "You wouldn't believe what some people are willing to pay for this stuff."

My mind flashed with an idea. A big one. I spun around and faced him. "Connor! You know what? Your family should donate something for my Thanksgiving baskets! We'd only need like twenty jars. Possibly thirty, if you could spare them. By Wednesday."

Connor started kissing my neck, and I closed my eyes and breathed. He'd shaved just before I got there. I knew because his cheeks were unbelievably smooth. That, and from the smell of his aftershave, woodsy and spicy and warm.

After a few kisses, I ducked out from underneath him. I couldn't let myself get sidetracked. I'd been slacking off on the Thanksgiving baskets. I'd been slacking off on everything. "Seriously, Connor. Are you listening to me?"

"I'm seriously distracted," he said, coming closer.

My hands went right to my hips. "There are a lot of

families in Liberty River who have nothing. They can't afford a Thanksgiving turkey, never mind all these fancy jellies. Don't you think you should give something back to people less fortunate than you? Isn't that only right?"

He nudged his chin in the direction of the shed. "Come on, Sterling. It's freezing."

I didn't move. And I didn't feel cold. I was starting to boil. "You know, it would be nice if you helped me out. Honestly, it's the least you could do."

He pulled the hood of his jacket up over his head. "What's that supposed to mean?"

"Well, let's see," I said, sarcastic. "You're not the one driving across town almost every night. You just roll out of bed and find me here, waiting. Your grades aren't suffering. You don't have to worry about falling asleep in your classes." Just hearing myself say these things out loud made me even madder. Connor looked at me blankly, like none of this had occurred to him before. I pointed at him. "You don't have to do any of the work or put in any effort to get something out of this arrangement."

Connor rubbed his hands together. The tips of his fingers were turning red with cold. "Are you saying you want me to sneak over to your place?"

"No, Connor!" That was the last thing I wanted —
to be with him someplace where we could actually get
caught. Connor didn't think about those things. He
didn't have to. "It's different for you. You don't have to
worry about college, keeping up your grades. I'm really
stressed out by this food drive. Stuff like that doesn't
magically come together. It takes hard work, effort, time.
And I need people to help me." I knew I sounded
annoyed with him, but why wouldn't Connor just agree
to get me some of this stuff for my baskets? Didn't he
want to help me?

He shook his head, wounded. "So basically, I should
give you a bunch of jellies because you come over here
to fool around with me? Like payment?"

"What? No! That's not what I'm saying!" Even
though maybe it was. All my muscles wound up tight,
from my toes up to my jaw. "And I really don't appreciate you insinuating as much. I'm not some slut from
school. You can't buy me off with jelly."

"Maybe you should go home," he said, drawing
curved lines in the gravel with the toe of his running
sneaker. "Call me crazy, but I don't see us having much
fun tonight."

I wanted to smack him. "Huh. That's funny! Because

about an hour ago, I said I shouldn't come over, but you talked me into it."

"I didn't talk you into anything, Sterling. That's a skill I definitely don't have."

"Oh? What's that's supposed to mean?" I asked. And then, I thought better of it. "You know what? Forget it. I'm leaving." I said it proud, like I didn't care. Pure, raw spite.

But as soon as I started walking back to my car, I felt sick. Connor let me go. He was going to let me drive away. He wasn't going to try to stop me. I wanted to turn around. I wanted to apologize, but I was too proud to do it.

I was fumbling for my keys when I heard him come up behind me.

"I'm sorry," he said. "I'm really stressed out, too. We've got playoffs this Wednesday, and our practices have sucked." He exhaled deeply. "Let's not fight."

"Yeah, well. It's a little late for that, huh?" I felt silly and desperate and immature, so much it made my palms sweat. I switched gears fast, to save face, to hide the fact that I expected Connor to care about me and my student council troubles. "And I wasn't trying to take advantage of you, by the way. I figured it would be good publicity for your family. The local paper is sending a photographer over to take pictures as we put the baskets together. I'd make it so the jars were prominently featured, and that your family got a special mention in the article."

I waited for Connor to say something, but he stayed quiet. Achingly quiet.

And then, before I knew what I was doing, I turned to face him and threaded my thumb through his belt loop. I suddenly wanted him to want me so bad that he'd do anything I said, give me anything I asked for. I wanted to have that power over Connor Hughes.

"I'll talk to my mom, okay? I can't promise anything, because like I said, it's expensive stuff, but I'll ask." I tried to say thank you, but my throat got tight. Connor took my hand, the one holding on to his pants, and tucked it in the warm pocket of his jacket. "It's getting late," he said.

I barely managed to nod.

But we both walked toward the shed anyway. Our sneakers crunched the gravel in sync until we were stepping on fallen pine needles, and then I couldn't hear anything at all.

CHAPTER THIRTY-TWO

Way too soon, it was time to put the Thanksgiving food baskets together. It should have been easy. Except I seemed to be the only one taking it seriously.

"Fire in the hole!" Ricky, one of the freshman reps, called through cupped hands, before launching a paper snowball in a high arc.

Another freshman rep, Phil, shouted, "That's what she said!"

The boys, squished together on a single mahogany library chair, cackled like hyenas, greasy faces beaming mischievous smiles. They tore out two more notebook sheets and wadded them up into fresh ammo.

"Guys!" I darted across the library, ducking my head. "Stop!"

While I'd been preoccupied getting the baskets prepped, Ricky and Phil had constructed a fort out of cranberry sauce cans, creamed corn cans, spinach cans. Nearly all the student donations had been stacked in pillars on top of their library table. They popped up over their tin wall every few seconds to launch attacks on a table of vulnerable boys across the library, who wildly swatted away the bombs with fat textbooks.

Sure, it was right before a holiday, and everyone was excited to have a couple of days off from school. But somehow, I'd lost control of student council. I thought back to my first meeting, and how I was so clearly the leader. How no one would dare speak unless I called on them first, how everyone respected me. Even feared me. It was the absolute opposite these days.

Ms. Bee emerged from the office, annoyed at the ruckus. She walked straight over to me. "Natalie. A moment, please."

"Yes, Ms. Bee?" I sounded a little annoyed, probably because I knew she was going to lay into me yet again. And yet again, I felt I deserved it.

"Things seem to be devolving here. Do you have a . . . a plan for this afternoon? Or are you flying by the seat of your pants?" Half her mouth wrinkled up.

"I — I'm trying to . . ."

Just then, Dave ran up and said, "Should I get every-one to start divvying up the food?"

"Yes," Ms. Bee and I said at the same time.

She glanced around the room, and I tried to keep my eyes up with hers. It was a disappointing sight.

"Is this all we have?" she asked.

"It will be enough," I said, even though I knew it wouldn't be. We needed to make twenty baskets, and there was barely enough food for ten. But what could I do? I'd tried my hardest to remind kids to bring in cans. I basically had to threaten the town grocery store into donating free turkeys. I was so happy when I convinced the bakery to give us loaves of bread, but I could tell when I'd picked them up this morning that they were already stale. Thanksgiving was tomorrow; they'd be rock hard by then.

I had wanted to give people a really nice Thanksgiving. A memorable one. I wanted my baskets to be something special and beautiful, like you'd see in one of those fancy home magazines. If this were the stuff that made up my Thanksgiving meal, I wouldn't feel much like celebrating. I'd probably kill myself.

"Doesn't this look great, everyone?" Spencer called out to the room, though her eyes were on Ms. Bee. She sat by herself at a nearby table, cutting big pieces of red gingham to line the willow tree baskets. "The fabric really dresses everything up. It was Natalie's idea."

While I appreciated what Spencer was trying to do, I felt stupid for spending money on the baskets and the fabric, especially when I could have bought more food for the families.

"Go ahead, Natalie," Ms. Bee said flatly. "Don't let me hold you up any further."

I sat down next to Spencer and, in the best possible penmanship I could muster, tried to write *Happy Thanksgiving* on little leaf-shaped paper tags. But my handwriting sucked. If Autumn had been there, she'd have been able to do it much better. She'd done most of my campaign signs.

My pen started to sputter, and I looked up to ask for another. That's when a balled up piece of paper hit me square in the face. A gasp told me it was an accident, and then the whole room quietly laughed, which made me want to kill whoever had thrown it. I glared at the boys and decided the offender in question was Phil, because out of everyone, his face was the reddest.

"Seriously, Phil. You're such a boner," Spencer shouted.

"Spencer!" I hissed. Ms. Bee was just across the room. "Shh."

Phil jabbed his finger though the air. "It wasn't me. Ricky did it!"

Ricky rushed the table. "Liar! Don't get me in trouble."

Ricky tried to wrestle Phil out from behind his fort, only to clip one of the towers. In the most incredible rumble, the cans came crashing down on the floor.

"Oh, my God!" I shouted, wading through the sea of metal. Cans were all over the place. Labels ripped. Some dented. A box of instant potatoes had broken open, spilling white flakes all over the floor. I sank to my knees, picked up two fistfuls and let it pour though my hands like sand.

"Boys!" Ms. Bee raced back over toward me. "Natalie! I need you to lead here."

"Excuse me, miss?"

I glanced up from the floor. A young man with a camera around his neck looked down at me.

"I'm here to take some pictures for the paper? Should I, uh, come back later?"

I bit my lip and held back tears as I got to my feet. That's when Connor appeared in the doorway, in a grass-stained football uniform that looked as if it hadn't been washed a single time this season, carrying an enormous cardboard box.

"Where should this go?" he called out to no one in particular.

Spencer came up next to me and squeezed my arm, reminding me to speak. "Anywhere," I said casually. "Anywhere is fine."

Five other uniformed JV players appeared behind Connor, also carrying boxes.

"What's in there?" the reporter asked, snapping a picture. Ms. Bee craned her neck from across the library.

Connor set his box down on a table and lifted the flaps. "I've got jellies and pie filling and fresh vegetables from our farm," Connor explained. And it was true. Oversize squash, zucchinis, carrots in bunches with long, ferny stems.

My cheeks burned. The boxes were absolutely stocked full. I wanted to cry again, but this time out of relief.

"You didn't have to do all this," I whispered when I got near enough. It took a lot of self-control to keep from throwing my arms around Connor and covering him with kisses.

"I know," Connor whispered back. He was grinning like a cat, and handed me a stack of green envelopes.

"What's this?"

"Coupons for free Christmas trees. I thought you could tuck them inside the baskets. If it doesn't go with the whole Thanksgiving thing, that's cool. Or, I don't know, if some people are Jewish or whatever. You don't have to use them."

"Connor. This is too much." As thrilled I was, I felt sick with guilt. After all, I'd practically forced him to do this for me. Connor's family made a lot of money off this stuff. There was at least several hundred dollars' worth of merchandise here.

"I told my mom about your project, and she wanted to help. Also," he whispered, "they're not for the expensive trees. Just the twenty-dollar spruces we sell to people who live in apartments. Only about this big." He put his hand at my nose. Playful and sweet.

Before I even knew what I was doing, I reached out to hug him. But I stopped, because Ms. Bee was watching me. Us. My arms dropped.

A flash of worry crossed his face, but he smiled through it. "I wanted to make sure you were getting something out of our arrangement." He was joking. But I couldn't bring myself to laugh. "I wanted to help you."

A football player came up behind him. "Shouldn't we get back to the locker room, before Coach Fallon makes us run extra laps?"

"Sure. Go on," Connor said. Then, as the younger boys took off, Connor leaned in close to me. I thought maybe he wanted a kiss, but instead he asked, "Will you come to the game? It's the championship tonight. Please?" I looked over his shoulder. Even though the rest of the student council kids were all busy unloading the boxes, I was sure they were noticing. I knew that Spencer was looking. She hadn't taken her eyes off Connor since he'd walked in. I took a big step back and started adjusting things on the table, keeping my distance.

"Thanks so much," I said. "We really appreciate your help." It came out stiff and formal.

Connor looked hurt for a second. Or maybe just confused. Then he turned and walked out.

I didn't have time to feel bad. Ms. Bee came over. "This stuff is wonderful," she admitted. But then she looked at me, kind of unforgiving. "That boy just saved you." She wasn't happy about it. She had wanted me to save myself.

After the baskets were finished, I walked over to the football game. It was already dark, and the floodlights lit up our field. The stands were full even though it was absolutely freezing outside. I knew Autumn was here. I'd seen her cuddled up under a blanket with other girls on my way over to the chain-link fence that ran the edge of the parking lot. I had my peacoat buttoned up, and I pulled my arms inside for extra warmth. My scarf was wrapped around my face, leaving just my eyes exposed. I couldn't feel my toes. I wanted to stay for the whole game for Connor, but it was freaking freezing.

Plus, we were losing. By a lot.

It was too far away to really see anyone, but since Connor was the QB, I could pick him out. It seemed like, with every single play, he'd get tackled. The ground was frozen, hard and unforgiving. Each time, I winced.

"I didn't think you liked football."

I turned to find Spencer holding two steaming cups of apple cider. I took one and said, "I don't."

"I'd watch competitive chess if that's what Connor Hughes wanted to play."

I kept my eyes on the field. There was no denying what Spencer had seen in the library today. "Please don't tell anyone."

"Of course I won't." The wind picked up, and Spencer pulled her furry jacket hood over her curls. "Why didn't you tell me that night at the diner?"

There were so many reasons, so I picked one at random. "I thought you liked him."

She laughed. "Natalie, please. I like *everyone*. I am very good at crushing. But seriously, what Connor did today was no joke." She jabbed her finger into my chest. "And you barely thanked him!"

Anger flickered up inside me. "What did you expect me to do, Spencer? Passionately kiss him? Offer him a gratis hand job? If I'd treated Connor differently than any other student who donated food, people would start to talk. And when people start talking . . . they don't stop. Trust me. Ms. Bee already suspects something. I know it."

Spencer looked at me like I was crazy. "Don't be paranoid, Natalie. Nobody knows anything. And all I'm saying is that you should do something nice for him."

"Do you *not* see me standing here, bored out of my mind and nearly freezing to death?"

Spencer laughed. "I hate to break it to you, but there's no way in hell Connor knows that you're here. You're not cheering for him, you're nowhere near our bleachers. You're practically standing in the parking lot."

I looked through a hole in the chain link like it was a telescope. "Connor knows," I said. "He knows I'm here."

Spencer didn't look convinced. And the more I thought about it, the less convinced I was, too. The only thing I felt sure of was that the cold wind suddenly felt much colder.

CHAPTER THIRTY-THREE

That night, Connor waited for me outside, blowing puffs of white out of his nose, like little empty thought balloons. I got out and we started walking to the shed. It was the coldest night yet. Frozen mud crunched underneath my feet.

"That was some battle, huh?"

"Funny that the one game you do show up at, we lose. I don't normally look that shitty out there." He sighed. "I can't believe the season's over. I'm never going to play football again."

I wrapped my mittened hand around his and pulled him to a stop.

Connor turned to face me. I looked at his house in the distance.

"Are you sure we won't get caught?" I was nervous, but smiling in spite of it. Mainly because I couldn't wait to see Connor's reaction.

He did not disappoint. His mouth dropped open the tiniest bit. "Seriously?"

"It's really cold," I said with a laugh. And it was. I wiped at my nose.

He gave my hand a squeeze. "Just stay close to me."

We sneaked up to the side of the house and entered through a back door into a pantry stocked with bags of rice, pastas, and glass jars filled with bright and bloated vegetables suspended in a yellowish water.

We passed his kitchen and slipped through a dining room with a big oak farm table with chipped white paint and an iron chandelier with tiny linen lampshades. The whole house smelled spicy and sweet, like a pumpkin pie with extra nutmeg and clove.

I felt exactly like I had that first night: giddy, nervous, excited, scared. All in a jumble.

When we reached the big staircase in the foyer, we stopped. Connor pointed down a hallway. "My parents' room," he whispered. And then he motioned for me to climb on his back.

"What?" This, I had not expected.

"The stairs are old and creaky. There should only be one set of footsteps."

He crouched down. I climbed as gracefully as I could up his spine. Which wasn't very graceful at all. You never think about how heavy you are until someone tries to pick you up. I felt like a sack of potatoes.

Connor sucked in a sharp breath.

"Are you okay?"

"Yeah. I just got knocked around pretty bad today." Connor put his arms behind his back and linked them underneath my butt for extra stability. It helped. And despite his injuries, Connor's strength surprised me. His steps sounded light and not at all lumbering as we creaked our way up to the second floor.

I rested my cheek against his flannel shirt and looked at all the family photos hanging on the wall. With each step up, Connor aged. He was a bright-eyed baby with so much brown hair, it almost looked like a toupee. Then Connor as a frowning kid, maybe seven, in a dress and covered with makeup, surrounded by four older girls who looked extremely entertained.

"Looks like your sisters were a couple of bullies," I whispered in his ear.

"Oh, yeah. They forced me to be their Barbie doll for years."

Then Connor got older, probably junior high, with the rope of an old sled over his shoulder, pulling two of his sisters, who were beautiful, through the snow.

Followed by Connor wearing an apron, helping his mom in the kitchen. Finally, there was recent Connor, the Connor who I clung to, standing next to his dad, each with an axe slung over his shoulder.

It felt like a time warp, catching up to this moment in fast motion. I was learning about Connor in a way I never had. I wanted to go slower, I wanted to linger on every picture.

When we reached the top of the stairs, I climbed down from his back. Braided rugs covered the wood floors. "My parents can't hear us now," he said, with such conviction that I couldn't help but think of the other girls he'd brought to his room, others he'd carried up the stairs, though I tried to push them out of my head. "Carlie and Corinne are home for Thanksgiving. I think they both went out with their old high school friends, but we should be quiet just in case."

When Connor put his hand on his doorknob, I realized that I hadn't thought much about what his room might look like. I made a quick guess of typical messy boyness — clothes on the floor, a pile of sports magazines, maybe a poster of a race car or a busty woman holding two frothy beer steins.

But Connor's room wasn't like that at all.

It was clean. Not just neat, but spotless. His mirror was streak-free, the beige carpet was vacuumed. His bookshelf had no books, but trophies of varying heights. They sparkled, free of dust. It smelled fresh, like laundry just out of a dryer, even though all his clothes were put away.

I took off my coat and hung it on the back of his desk chair. There was a stack of papers in a pile — spreadsheets crowded with numbers and figures, thicker than my AP Calc textbook.

"What are these?" I asked.

"Business plans, budgets, projections for next year." Connor sat down on his bed. I sat next to him. "I can't believe you're here," he said.

"Why? You've had plenty of girls in here before."

I regretted saying it. Because I didn't want to think about Connor with other girls, and because of the way Connor had gotten mad at me for bringing up how he'd lost his virginity. This time, though, he wasn't angry. He looked at me deeply and said, "Never a girl like you."

And it didn't sound corny, and it didn't sound like a line or a lie, or any of the things I would have assumed when we first got together. Things were different now.

I was different, ready to accept Connor for who he really was — a good guy who wouldn't do anything to hurt me. The realization that I implicitly, unconditionally trusted him overwhelmed me with warmth.

Connor reached to turn his lamp off, but I guided his arm away. I wasn't scared of the light, of what Connor was about to see. I didn't want to hide anymore.

He looked up at me with wide, almost disbelieving eyes as I lifted off my T-shirt and shimmied out of my pants. I unhooked my bra and slid down my underwear. I could tell Connor saw me the way I wanted to be seen. As beautiful, as strong. I expected to be nervous, but I felt confident in a way I never had in the shed. The moment was so different than what I'd imagined. There was no fear, no embarrassment. It was pure liberation.

I took Connor's clothes off, too. His body was bruised. Wounded. Fragile. I lay down next to him and touched him extra gently. But I had to touch him. When I did, my hands were suddenly too small. They couldn't feel enough of him, hold enough of his skin. I didn't want any space in between our bodies. No light, no air, but a vacuum. I rolled on top of him and let gravity press us together. Lips, chest, abdomen, thighs.

I wasn't planning to have sex with him. Only now it was all I wanted. My body and my mind and all my parts shouted that this was the right thing to do right now. I needed to be with Connor. I was in love with him.

And that sudden clarity triggered an avalanche. I felt overcome with the freedom of feeling the feelings I'd worked so hard to hide. I stopped talking myself out of what I desperately wanted.

"Do you have something we could use?" I whispered.

"Wait." He pushed my hair so it fell over one shoulder. "This isn't because of today, is it? The Thanksgiving baskets? Because I don't want it to be like that."

I could have cried. I'd pushed Connor away for so long, he had no idea how deeply I cared about him. My feelings had been locked up in that shed because I was afraid to let them out. Except now, for whatever reason, I wasn't scared to show him how I felt. It was the only thing I wanted to do. "It's not like that."

Sex is something we learn about in abstract, clinical concepts. Condoms come with instructions, health class provides textbook illustrations of parts and procedures. I'd known how things were supposed to go, the actions, what would physically happen between us. But the thing I'd never understood were how brightly the feelings would spark. The absolute euphoria of knowing that

Connor and I couldn't physically get any closer to each other.

Connor kept quietly asking if I was okay. He seemed more unsure than I was, his quivering hands holding on to me, like he was off balance. He had more experience than I did, but I could tell that what we were doing was different from what he'd had with any other girl before.

The entire world fell away until it was just me and Connor.

Finally.

CHAPTER THIRTY-FOUR

I woke up to the morning sun on my face and Connor's arm draped across my chest. For a second, it felt like the best thing ever.

And then I shot up.

Connor lifted his head, glanced at the clock, and cursed under his breath.

I was already standing, putting my clothes back on. My underwear and my bra were cold from having spent the night on the floor. I could barely look at Connor. It wasn't regret. Not exactly. But all the wonderful feelings from the night before had been replaced by dread. There was no way an accident like this could have happened in our shed. It was too cold, too uncomfortable. Maybe for a reason.

"I've got to get out of here," I said. "How do I get out of here?" I knew I sounded panicked and crazy. And I was. Absolutely. I needed to get back to my house before my parents noticed I was missing.

Connor opened his bedroom door a crack. He sniffed out in the hallway. "My mom's already cooking."

Shit. It was Thanksgiving. We usually went to my Aunt Doreen's house, but Mom always woke up early to make a pie.

"I need to go. Now."

Connor raked his hands through his hair. "Okay. Here's what we'll do. I'll carry you downstairs. Then I'll go into the kitchen and distract my mom while you leave through the front door."

My heart wilted. This wasn't at all fun or exciting, like it used to be to sneak out to the shed. I finished getting dressed while Connor put on sweats and a T-shirt. We didn't speak to each other. Connor seemed too tired for words, and I was too wide awake to be able to choose from the thousands that were swirling with alarm in my head.

As Connor carried me down the stairs, I could hear his mother whistling from the kitchen. And apparently she could hear him, too.

"Connor?" she called out.

He stopped and I felt both of our hearts pounding together.

"Yeah, Mom?"

"You're up early."

"I smelled your cooking."

"Well, pancakes are just about ready. Go wake up your sisters and your father."

Connor let me down when we reached the bottom step. The front door stood a few feet away. "Okay," he whispered. "Listen, I —"

"I'll text you later," I whispered back, then pushed him toward the kitchen.

Connor disappeared around a corner, and I stayed still until I heard him talking to his mom. Then I tip-toed to the front door and pulled it open. Or at least, I tried. But it was locked. I fiddled a hundred combinations with the dead bolt and the latch on the knob, and kept pulling as hard as I could.

A toilet flushed. Upstairs, where Connor's sisters were supposed to be sleeping. My hand was cold and clammy on the brass knob. I heard footsteps descending the stairs behind me.

The lock finally clicked and I pulled the door open. The cold slapped me in the face. That and the bright-ness. It had snowed about a foot overnight. White reflected everywhere.

I stepped outside and closed the door behind me

harder than I intended to. The brass knocker tapped a few times.

I took off running to my car, leaving footsteps in the snow, evidence the whole way. Snow soaked into my pant legs, burned my ankles. My car was covered. I pulled my hands inside my coat and wiped off just enough so I could see. Then I jumped inside and turned on the car and hit the gas, my hands, my face, everything stinging red.

As I turned down the driveway, I glanced back up at the house. Mrs. Hughes stood on the front porch, watching me go.

Usually when I left Connor's house, I felt better than before I'd come. But not this time.

My cell buzzed in the cup holder. I thought maybe it was Connor, but it was my parents. I scrolled through my call history. My home number filled up every single slot since five in the morning.

I pulled over on the side of the road, cleaned off the rest of my windshield, and let the heater warm up. I tried to come up with a plan. My thoughts kept creeping back to what I'd done with Connor, flashes of skin and rushes of heat. But instead of enjoying the memories, I was imagining lies to cover the fact that it had happened.

○ ○ ○

My parents sat together on the couch, watching one of those 24-hour news channels. I didn't know if they were looking for *Breaking News: Local Girl Found Dead in Ditch*. They looked paler, older than I'd ever seen them.

"I'm so sorry," I said.

They both rushed to me. Pulling at me, hugging me, and checking me over. My mom was crying. My dad had his jaw set, tears in his eyes. The way they looked at me, it made me want to vomit. How much I'd let them down. How terribly I'd worried them.

The goodwill of me simply being alive wore away quickly. They demanded to know where the hell I'd been.

"I was at Autumn's house. I fell asleep."

"I thought you weren't talking to Autumn." Mom's voice was strange. She didn't exactly believe me, but I could tell she wanted to. And I was in luck: Because of my fight with Autumn, apparently Mom hadn't called over there to look for me.

"We . . . we made up. I called her last night to finally talk things over. And Autumn invited me over so we could do it in person. We cried a lot. It was exhausting, and I ended up falling asleep over there. I'm really, really sorry."

I hadn't noticed that I was crying, but I was. Because I was lying, and because I wanted my lie to be the truth.

I got one last hug from each of them before I was grounded.

CHAPTER THIRTY-FIVE

Connor texted me a bunch of times over the rest of the Thanksgiving holiday. They started out really apologetic and concerned. Messages like sorry and were your parents awake?

I texted back I'm fine. And then I turned my phone off.

I wished I could turn myself off, too. I could barely look at my parents. Not after how easily I'd lied to them. I was a terrible liar, but they ate it up. What other choice did they have? They didn't want to think that their daughter was capable of doing the things I'd done. I didn't want to think I was capable of them, either.

As right as sleeping with Connor had felt, the realization about how other people would judge what I'd done spoiled everything. I was okay in the shed, hidden in Connor's bedroom. When it was just us operating in a judgment-free zone.

Except there was no such place in real life. The addition of everyone else in my life threw Connor and me off balance.

I didn't turn my phone on again until Monday homeroom. My voicemail box was full of hang-ups. The texts from Connor flooded in. Eleven of them. His tone changed with each one, sounding slightly more desperate.

Just let me know you're okay.

And angry.

Why are u ignoring me?

And defensive.

I DIDN'T DO ANYTHING!

He was right. He hadn't. I'd done it all.

I first noticed people talking during lunch. I was in line at the cafeteria. Autumn, Marci, and a couple of other girls were discussing something in fevered whispers. They were so captivated, they didn't even notice that they were totally blocking the registers.

I made a big show of huffing and puffing as I squeezed between them and the chip rack to get by. I even said, "Excuse me," in a snotty way, because I was so annoyed about my pizza. You can never get hot pizza at school. Those red heating lamps don't do jack. You've got literally five minutes to eat your slice, and it will be lukewarm at best. Longer than that, and you're out of luck.

As I pushed past them, Autumn stopped whispering to give me a look. It wasn't a bitchy look, exactly. More like one of confirmation, a knowing look. Like I was involved somehow in whatever story they were all talking about.

That's when I started to get nervous. Had Connor told people about what we'd done? As a punishment for not texting him back? I knew he was mad at me, but I couldn't believe he'd do something like that.

I spent the rest of the day watching people talk. By eighth period, it was clear Ross Academy was entirely abuzz over something extremely juicy. It seemed to be the kind of gossip that literally catches fire, transcending cliques and loyalties. The same thing had happened last year, when Walter Desmon got a huge boner in swim class and refused to get out of the pool for fifteen minutes.

I lurked just inside the door of the library, partially enveloped in the folds of a big American flag. If I craned my head until my neck hurt, I could see down the hall to where Dipak, Martin, and David were huddled together whispering. My ears rang, I tried that hard to eavesdrop.

"Natalie?" Susan Choi popped up in front of me. "Umm, did you want the tables pushed together? Or did you want them, like, in rows?"

"Whatever," I said, rising up to my toes so I could see over her head. "You choose."

"Cool!" Susan said, then sprinted back to the rest of the students who'd come in for the meeting. "Okay! Natalie says that we can choose how to arrange the tables today. So . . . should we take a vote?"

Now there was too much noise in the library to hear the conversation down the hall, so I focused below Martin's spotty mustache and tried to read his lips. It proved completely unnecessary, though, because all three heads suddenly snapped back. The boys shouted *Whoa!* and gasped for air in between deep laughs.

My stomach seized. Sure, I'd had these kind of panic attacks ever since Connor and I got together. Only this time, I wasn't just being paranoid. The realization made my legs quiver as the boys made their way into the library. And it didn't go unnoticed that none of them could make eye contact with me as they walked past.

Susan popped back out of the room. "Natalie?" She bit her lip and glanced around. "Can I talk to you for a second? Before the meeting?"

"What, Susan?"

"There's something I want to tell you." She exhaled so hard it fluttered her bangs. "There's a naked picture of Spencer making the rounds on everyone's cell phones."

I almost couldn't believe my ears. "Are you kidding?"

Susan grimaced. "I thought you'd want to know, since you're friends with her."

I felt so many things. Embarrassment for Spencer. Anger. Disappointment. It reminded me of the moment Autumn had told me about her and Chad Rivington, when I couldn't believe that a friend of mine could be so stupid.

More than anything, though, I felt utter relief that it wasn't me people were talking about. That somehow I had, miraculously, dodged this bullet.

"Does Spencer know?" I asked.

Susan shook her head. "I'm not sure. I saw her sitting in some junior guy's lap at lunch, picking the sweet peppers off his hoagie. But if she doesn't, she will soon. Everyone's phones are blowing up."

I shook my head. "I wonder if she knows who took the picture."

Susan shrugged. "Maybe. Unless she does this kind

of thing all the time." The implication of her words hung in the air. "I think it's been forwarded and refor-warded so many times by this point, it's going to be difficult to figure out." Her lip curled. "It's really disgusting."

I stared down at Susan. She seemed horribly judg-mental for someone who completely idolized Spencer a few weeks ago. Then again, that's how quickly people's perceptions could change. It only took one mistake, one stupid decision.

"If you want to see it, you could ask Dipak. It's on his phone. He showed it to me." She sounded almost proud.

"I don't want to see a naked picture of Spencer," I said. "And I don't think other people should be looking at it, either."

"It's a little too late for that," Susan said. "By the end of our meeting, you'll probably be the only person left in school who hasn't seen it."

Spencer didn't show up for the student council meeting. I wasn't surprised. The whole meeting, people kept checking their phones, as if they were hoping more pho-tos might pop up.

After the meeting, I walked straight to my car and called Connor. I was half-afraid he wouldn't pick up, but he did on the second ring. He picked up and started yelling at me.

"Where have you been? I've been calling you all weekend!"

"We need to talk."

"Oh, so we only talk when you decide we need to?" He was really pissed.

"I'm sorry. I don't know. I've . . ." I trailed off. "Where can we meet?"

"People are going to be at the farm. We opened for Christmas the day after Thanksgiving." He sighed. "I had to bring the sleeping bag and everything inside."

Our shed was gone. It felt like a Band-Aid had been ripped off. Cruel, but necessary. "I don't want to go to your house," I said, picturing his mother, staring at me from the front porch.

I could hear him thinking. "There's a little dirt road before my house. On the left. It's just a turnaround spot. I'll be there in ten minutes."

"I didn't think it was possible for our meet-ups to get any shadier." I meant it as a joke — a bad joke, because things were so awkward, and I wanted something to make things feel less tense.

I could hear the disapproval in his silence. And then he hung up.

I had a bad feeling driving over, and it got worse when I climbed out of my car. Connor leaned against the bumper of his pickup truck. He couldn't look at me. And I couldn't look at him.

Of all things, I thought about Adam and Eve. How they'd been so happy, playing naked in the garden. And then in one moment, it all turned to shame. They couldn't have even known what was happening. They'd never known anything but joy. And then suddenly, there was hesitation. Silence. Awkwardness. Everything was ruined.

We stood in the snow and stared at each other's toes. I could feel him trying to muster up the courage to say something. So I made sure to say something first.

"Well, have you seen it?" I asked.

He was completely confused. "Have I seen *what?*"

"The picture of Spencer."

"Maybe. Unless that's going to get me in even more trouble."

I smacked him on the arm. "This isn't funny. Did you just see it, or do you have it?"

He pulled his phone out from his pocket. I reached for it, but he lifted it high over his head.

"Come on. Let me see!"

"Why do you want to?"

"Because she's my friend."

"Then you probably shouldn't see it."

My heart fell. "Just show me."

He tapped a few buttons, and then passed me the phone.

Nothing could have prepared me for seeing Spencer like this on the tiny pixelated screen. Her curls, her puckered lips, her bare breasts cast forward toward the cameraman.

My mind flashed back to that summer I'd baby-sat her.

She had wanted to dance through the sprinklers and so I told her to get her bathing suit on. The only one that wasn't dirty was one from the summer before, when Spencer was a lot shorter.

A couple of the neighborhood boys had come to play in the sprinklers, too. And it wasn't until Spencer came up to me, dripping wet and begging for a popsicle, that I noticed. The straps dug deep in her shoulders, the front dipped too low. It barely covered her. You could see everything.

The kids were all innocent then. They didn't notice or care. But I was uncomfortable, because I knew better. I ran inside and made Spencer put on a T-shirt. And when I did, I felt like I was taking something away from her, instead of covering her up.

I forced myself to look at the photo again. Spencer thought she was sexy, but it just made me sad. She wasn't powerful, in control. She wasn't anything she thought she was.

I went to hand the phone back, but something caught my eye. Spencer held a wad of fabric up at her neck. I recognized it instantly. Her plaid nightgown. Behind her were a bunch of lab desks, a cabinet full of glass beakers. And suddenly, I knew who took the picture.

"Mike Domski."

"What?"

"Mike took this picture."

Connor looked at me blankly, like I didn't know what I was talking about.

"Look," I said, "I saw him the night of the sleepover, coming out of the science lab with a shit-eating grin on his disgusting face. I know he did it."

"You can't tell anyone about this, Sterling."

"Says who?" I started walking toward my car.

Connor grabbed hold of my arm. "Please. Don't get involved."

"Why not?"

He dropped his head back. "I don't know. Because

Spencer kind of had it coming, after what she did to Mike in the theater? Because Spencer can do what she wants to do? Because it's none of your business?"

I couldn't believe Connor was saying this. It was as if he'd pulled off the mask that I always suspected he was wearing. "Are you kidding me?"

"Seriously. Spencer's going to do what she's going to do. You're not in charge of her. If she wants to tell someone, it's up to her. Not you."

I stared at Connor. "How could I have not seen that you are as big of a dick as Mike Domski?"

"You're angry. I understand that. But don't take it out on me. I'm trying to protect you."

"What does that even mean? I don't need you to protect me. I can protect myself."

"You know what I think? You're using Spencer as an excuse not to deal with what's going on with us."

"What *is* going on with us, Connor? We're having fun, right? Fun, fun, fun. Well, you know what? I'm not having fun anymore. Not when I have to lie to my parents, not when I have to give up my life so you and I can mess around. I'm tired of messing around. It only leaves a mess. Because this is what happens — don't you see?" I handed back his phone. "It stops being fun, and it starts being other things. Like hurt. And gossip. And judgment. And blame. You might not care about that. And lord knows Mike Domski doesn't. But I do. I know you don't want me to confront him, but you know what? It feels like I've been waiting for this moment my whole life."

"Sterling, don't —"

His words hit my back, because I was already gone. And anyway, it was way too late for *don't*. Because we already had.

CHAPTER THIRTY-SIX

Spencer didn't answer any of my phone calls that night, obviously avoiding me. I drove to her apartment complex, but I couldn't remember which building I'd dropped her off at.

When I went to school the next morning, I camped out at her locker. I sat right on the floor until homeroom bell. Only she never showed up.

I went to AP Chemistry and took my seat. It was across the room from where Spencer had taken her now-infamous photo. It made me sick to stare at that open space, to think about what she'd done there with Mike Domski. I knew she wouldn't want to talk to me about it, but I didn't care.

"Mr. Quinn? May I use the bathroom?"

He looked annoyed at my outburst, but nodded toward the oxygen molecule hall pass.

I walked toward the main office. Principal Hurley was there, leaning over his secretary's desk. I waited to enter until he went into his office and closed the door.

"Excuse me," I said to the secretary in my most polite voice. "But could you tell me if Spencer Biddle was marked present today? I . . . uh, have to give her a special student council message and I haven't been able to find her."

"Spencer was suspended this morning." The secretary leaned in close to the small fern flanking her desk and whispered, "Principal Hurley became aware of a picture."

Damn. "When?"

"About fifteen minutes ago."

I sprinted out to the parking lot. And when Spencer wasn't there, I climbed into my car. I had to drive around a little before I found her a few blocks from school, waiting to cross the street. I pulled over to the side of the road and put my hazards on.

"Come on," I said. "Get in."

Spencer didn't look at me. "I'm fine. Thanks anyway."

"Spencer. Don't be a baby. Let me drive you home."

After a big sigh, she walked toward the car and leaned down to my window. "I don't want a lecture from you, okay? Because I really don't care. I honestly think the way everyone's getting worked up is funny."

"Funny? Suspension is funny?"

"A week's suspension is no big deal."

"It will be when you start looking for colleges! I mean, I'm still haunted by a C-plus I got in Home Ec sophomore year."

"Well, I'm not planning to go to Harvard, so I'm sure I'll be fine."

I was fuming. She was clearly putting on an act. "I know who took the picture, Spencer. I know it was Mike Domski."

The bravado melted from her face. It was the first time that I saw the little girl, the one I used to babysit. "It was not," she lied.

"It was, too, Spencer! I saw him sneaking out of the labs that night. And you were wearing pajamas in the picture." Ugh. I wanted to throw up, thinking of her with him. "You knew what kind of an a-hole Mike was. Why would you do something so stupid? And why in God's name would you *ever* cover for him?"

"The picture was just a part of my plan to get him to drop his pants at the theater. I had to make him think I was interested. He's just trying to get me back. I thought it was over, but then . . ."

"What?"

"That pinky wave thing I made up. Everyone's been doing it. Not just the girls, but boys, too. This one freshman guy did it yesterday morning, and I thought Mike was going to explode. I guess that was the final straw. Honestly, I thought he deleted the picture. That's what he'd told me, anyway."

"So get him back! Tell on him!"

"Natalie, stay out of it."

"If you're going to be in trouble for this, then he should be, too, right? I mean, isn't that only fair? He took advantage of you, Spencer."

"I wanted to pose for the picture. He didn't force me."

"And that gives Mike free rein to exploit you? Spencer, you're in trouble because of what he did."

She brushed her hair back. "Look, it's over. Mike and I are even. I just want it to go away."

I laughed. "Go away? You're being passed around school like a trading card! Don't you have any self-respect?"

"Of course I do," her voice was sharp. Of all people for her to be mad at, she was getting mad at me.

"Haven't you learned anything from what I've taught you? You're better than this, Spencer!"

She started laughing. "I love how you're basically

calling me a slut, but you're doing the exact same thing with Connor."

Now the edge was in my voice. "It's not the same thing."

"You're letting Connor Hughes use you. Or you're using him. Whatever. Either way, you're a big phony. You play like you're so good and that just because you fool around with Connor in secret, you're somehow better than me. It's easier for you to be mad at me, instead of at yourself."

"I am nothing like you, Spencer. Nothing."

"Just leave me alone. You're not my babysitter anymore."

"Well, that's too bad, because you could really use one!"

I had enough. I was supposed to be in class, anyway. Spencer could walk home in the cold for all I cared.

I pulled away, and vowed that I wasn't going to get involved any further. If Spencer wanted to destroy her life, so be it. But then, later that day, I saw Mike Domski at lunch, grinning like the Cheshire cat as people clamored to look at his cell phone. Suddenly, I understood why Spencer didn't tell. If she kept Mike out of it, the naked picture would be something she was okay with. But naming Mike, telling on him for what he'd done, would signal she actually *did* have a problem with it. And then suddenly, just like that, Spencer would be a victim. It was not a role she wanted to play.

Or maybe it was more simple than that. Maybe Spencer just didn't have the guts to stand up to Mike Domski. Because the Mike Domskis of the world usually won.

Either way, I knew I had to do the right thing. And I had to hope that Spencer would thank me later for it.

CHAPTER THIRTY-SEVEN

As soon as I finished eating, I headed for Principal Hurley's office. His secretary said he was busy, but I ignored her and opened his door.

"Let me call you back," he said, and set his phone on the cradle.

I didn't even wait for him to ask me what I was doing there. I just came right out and said, "I know who took that naked photo of Spencer. It was Mike Domski."

He leaned forward and said in this ridiculously helpless voice for a principal, "What do you suggest I do?"

Wasn't it obvious? "Mike should be held accountable in the same way Spencer was. One week's suspension."

Principal Hurley shook his head. "Spencer is the one who broke the rules here. Spencer is the one who disrobed."

"Yes, but —"

"And I am sure that Mike Domski wasn't the only one to forward the photograph."

"Well, of course, but —"

"I'm certainly not about to conduct a witch hunt, trying to find out everyone who was involved."

"I'm not saying you should. But like I just told you, Mike Domski was the one who started it all. He took the picture."

"Perhaps he did. But it will be your word against his, since Spencer refused to implicate her photographer. And anyway, Spencer was the one who chose to expose herself on school property. Otherwise, there would be nothing to take a picture of."

I could barely sit still. "So that's it? You're going to suspend Spencer, but Mike doesn't get so much as a slap on the wrist?"

"I'll have a talk with him," Principal Hurley offered. "Though I doubt he will confess. Now, do you need a pass back to class?"

I did not need a pass. I walked straight out and down to Ms. Bee's office. Except she wasn't there. She was teaching. I paced the halls and finally found her classroom.

I knocked on the door and summoned her out. She looked shocked by my disruption to say the least.

"Yes?"

"Mike Domski sent around a naked picture of

Spencer. She got suspended, but nothing happened to him. And it is completely, totally unfair."

Ms. Bee closed the classroom door. "Natalie. Breathe. Now, what's going on?" I did what she told me to. I breathed. And then I repeated everything slowly.

When I was done, she asked, "How do you know it was him?"

"Because Spencer's wearing the pajamas that she had on at girls' night. And you can tell the picture was taken in the science lab, which is exactly where I found Mike Domski hiding."

She frowned. "I'm not following." Except she *was* following.

And then I realized that I was going to be in trouble, too.

"Some boys snuck into the girls' night, after you fell asleep. I tried to chase them out. I didn't want to upset you. I handled it."

"Oh? Did you?" Ms. Bee shook her head. It looked like I'd only managed to delay the upset. "Natalie, you're lucky that you haven't been officially implicated in this. Principal Hurley might suspend you, too."

Maybe Ms. Bee was right, but Spencer was my friend. I had to defend her. "Please. You have to help."

"What I have to do is get back to my class."

"You have influence over Principal Hurley. You could tell him that Mike should be held equally responsible. He'd listen to you. I know he would."

"Natalie, someone like Spencer needs to learn that her actions have consequences. You tried to help her after those ridiculous Rosstitute shirts, and I supported you on that. But I'm afraid this time, she's going to have to suffer her punishment, whatever Principal Hurley decides." She wiped at a bead of sweat on her forehead. "I will certainly see that Mr. Domski's participation is investigated. But that won't let your friend off the hook. Now get back to class immediately, or I'm going to have to write you up."

CHAPTER THIRTY-EIGHT

You'd think I would have figured it out a little quicker. After all, I'd seen it happen before to Autumn. And then, just two days earlier, to Spencer. But it took about halfway through the Wednesday before I realized that everyone was talking about me.

Granted, I was in a fog. I'd given up hope that Mike would be brought to any real justice. And I knew that once Spencer found out that I'd stuck my nose into her business, she'd probably never talk to me again. Connor and I weren't speaking. Ms. Bee thought I was a moron for standing up for Spencer and, even worse, for letting boys into girls' night. And my friendship with Autumn felt like a distant memory.

It turned out that Principal Hurley was true to his word. Maybe he realized that taking pictures of under-age naked girls was illegal — so he wanted to get involved before the police did. Who knows? But he called Mike into his office for a stern talking to. Mike denied everything, of course. And, really, how could it be proven? The photo was texted to so many cell phones, it was impossible to determine where it had originated from. And none of the boys at school would out Mike Domski.

Principal Hurley must have mentioned there was a witness, because when Mike left that office, he knew I was involved. And he didn't waste any time in getting his revenge.

I was packing up my books after school when Mike walked right up to my ear and whispered, "I know all about you. About what you do with Connor. I've known since the first night you snuck over his place, you stupid little nympho."

I'd never been scared of Mike Domski before. But at that moment, I trembled.

"I don't know what you're talking about," I managed to say.

"He's my best friend, bitch. You think he hasn't told me everything? I practically know what you look like naked."

There was no dignified exit to take. So I just ran. I left my locker door open and dropped my books on the floor and I ran.

In a way, I did save Spencer. Her naked picture was

only infamous for about forty-eight hours, before the torch was passed to me.

I stayed home sick the next day, thinking it might temper things down. In fact, the opposite happened. Without me there, no one had to whisper.

Friday was the most awful day of my whole life.

It started with Connor walking up to my locker. I got there really early to avoid people. But he'd gotten there earlier.

"Please," I told him. "Leave me alone. I don't want anyone to see us talking."

He looked like he hadn't slept, in the same way I hadn't slept. He looked haunted, in the same way I was haunted. He looked mad, in the same way I was devastated.

"You are unbelievable," he said, launching right into me.

I launched right back. "I told you I didn't want anyone to know what we were doing! And of all people, you told Mike?"

"Mike is my best friend. He didn't say anything about it until you tried to get him in trouble! I told you not to get involved."

"Oh, so am I the wrong one here? Mike takes naked photos of a *fourteen-year-old girl* and spreads them to *the whole school,* and *I'm* the one who did something wrong? Is that what you're saying?"

"No. Believe me. I want to kill Mike right about now. It's just that . . ."

"What? It's just that *what*?"

"Look, I wish he hadn't done it. I really wish he hadn't."

"And I wish that Spencer had kept her freaking boobs covered up. But I also wish you wouldn't protect Mike, and I wish that the whole school didn't think I'm a slut. I trusted you to keep it between us, and you didn't. You let everyone into our private world. I thought you cared enough about me to never let that happen."

It was the first time I'd seen him so angry. His forehead crinkled up, and one vein became really prominent. He had his hands clenched.

But I was just as mad. Madder, even. "I never wanted any of this. In fact, I never wanted anything to do with you! I knew that you —"

"Save it, Sterling. I'm not going to force you to stoop to my level." He said the last part sarcastic.

"I told you we needed to keep things quiet from the very beginning. So don't make me out to be the bad person here. It's my reputation that's been damaged. Everyone's laughing at me, not you!" I was screaming, shaking. How could Connor not see? He escaped from this whole thing unscathed. He had another notch in his belt. But me, I was a joke.

"I'm sorry. I know everything sucks for you right now. But can't you see that's your own fault."

I laughed. "You're really great at this cheering up stuff. Thanks so much for making me feel better."

"You're the one who made it seem like we were doing something wrong. Maybe you still feel like that, because for whatever reason, you think I'm not good enough for you. But I like you, okay? I've liked you from the very beginning."

"It was never going to go anywhere."

"Because you wouldn't let it go anywhere. Look, I know you've got a million and one reasons. I hear you. Most of them are true. We're probably not going to be a couple after graduation. You'll leave Liberty River, and I'll be here. I get it. But you know what? I liked you anyway. I let myself have feelings for you despite not knowing how this would end."

He turned like he was going to walk away, but then thought better of it. "I'm done trying to convince you of who I am and why I'm worthy of you. And you can spin that however you want. Go ahead and make me the bad guy, so you can be the good girl. Except deep down, I know that you don't believe that's the way things are for a second."

"It's too late," I whispered. To him? To myself? I wasn't sure.

He heard. "It's only too late because you're saying it's too late."

I said it again. "It's too late."

It was only after he was gone that I started to cry. It was only when everyone else started showing up for school that I felt completely alone.

It was crazy, the weight of everyone's eyes on me. Their looks actually felt heavy; they made it hard for me to pick up my legs. I thought about Autumn, and how I thought I'd protected her from this. But I didn't have a clue what it was really like, how terribly cruel and mean and judgmental people could be.

I ran to the girls' bathroom near the teacher's lounge, for an escape. I cried right there at the sink. I felt pathetic, *student council president turned closet slut*. It was too perfect — the kind of story that people loved to tell.

I had to accept this. As much as I wanted to blame Mike and Connor and Spencer, it was my fault I was in this situation. I'd known better than to get involved with someone like Connor. I'd known the risks, and I'd done it anyway. Except that what everyone thought of me didn't even come close to how badly I thought of myself.

I grabbed a paper towel and wiped my face. It was so rough, like sandpaper. My whole face was red and blotchy and swollen. I ducked my head and splashed it with some cold water.

When the faucet was turned off, I heard a voice, unmistakable, through the vents over my head.

Ms. Bee.

"I didn't think she was that kind of girl." I scampered up onto the ledge and strained to listen. "I overheard two of my students talking about her in homeroom yesterday. I would have never thought Natalie would do something like that. Then again, she's been acting out big-time. Fraternizing with that Spencer girl."

I closed my eyes to stop the room from spinning. What would have ever made me think that teachers wouldn't hear about this, too? After all, it was all over the school.

Another teacher agreed. "Natalie always seemed like such a nice girl."

But I am *a nice girl*, I wanted to scream.

"I know. That's the worst thing. I thought she was something special. I put a lot of my own time and attention into her for nothing." Ms. Bee sighed a deep, painful sigh. "And Connor Hughes, of all people. You'd think she'd be smarter than that. I feel heartbroken over the whole thing."

I had to get out of that bathroom, or else I was going to puke. I wanted to defend myself, but I knew Ms. Bee was right. I should have been smarter. I should have been a lot of things.

I had always known what kind of girl I was . . . until I didn't.

CHAPTER THIRTY-NINE

I'd hoped that the weekend would have made everything blow over, but of course it didn't. People were still talking about me on Monday. Rightfully so, I supposed. By Monday after school, it was clear what I needed to do.

I spent my lunch period in my car, working on my letter of resignation for Ms. Bee. In the first draft, I said way too much. About how disappointed in myself I was. The whole big long sorry story of me and Autumn. How I'd messed up with Connor. I poured my heart out. You could tell by the tearstains and the terrible penmanship.

Except when I reread it, it made me sick. I was groveling for her forgiveness. I was making excuses, when really, I had no one to blame but myself. It was childish. And I knew Ms. Bee would think so, too.

I made my next draft a single sentence long.

Though it has been a pleasure working with you,
I hope you'll accept my resignation effective
immediately.
  Sincerely
  Natalie Sterling

I slipped it under her office door.

I'd thought resigning would make me feel better.

It didn't.

After school, I went to my locker. The agenda for today's student council meeting was to finalize plans for the ceremony when my portrait would be hung on the library wall, and to address and mail the invitations Ms. Bee had printed. I'd quit just in time so the event could be canceled.

I got my books, closed my locker door, and there was Spencer, holding my resignation letter.

"What the hell is this, Natalie?"

"Where'd you get that?" I snatched it out of her hands.

"Where do you think? I went to Ms. Bee's office to hand in assignments from my suspension. I saw you sliding it under her door. Thank God I scooped it up before she found it."

I could have strangled her. "Do you have any idea what you've done? They're mailing the portrait ceremony invitations today. Now I look even more irresponsible for not showing up!"

Spencer was unmoved. "You can't quit student council, Natalie. You're the president!"

"I can too," I said, and stormed down the hall.

Spencer kept pace. "Natalie, you were right. What I did with Mike was stupid. I wanted to pretend like I didn't care. And you know what? Before you, I *wouldn't* have cared. But now I do."

"I'm very happy for you."

"And here's what else I know." She grabbed my arm and made me look at her. "You stuck up for me when no one else would. And you did the same thing for Autumn. Which begs the question . . . When will you start sticking up for yourself?"

I shook my head. "It's not that easy, Spencer! I can't even look at Ms. Bee, never mind everyone else at school. I actually had to hear Ms. Bee in the bathroom, saying the most awful things about me. And they were true, Spencer. They were all true."

"They are not, and you know it. Quit feeling sorry for yourself."

"I do feel sorry for myself! I'm mortified. You were

right, okay? I built myself up to this impossible standard and I failed. I failed miserably."

"That's fine, so long as it's your judgment and not someone else's."

"All right. I'll just magically forget that the entire school thinks I'm a hypocritical slut and answer to myself. Hmm. Let's see. I've messed everything up with Connor. With Autumn. With Ms. Bee. With you." Even though I was trying to be sarcastic, tears filled my eyes.

"So that's the problem? Not the sex."

I had to think about it for a second. Sure, the reality that everyone at Ross Academy was judging what I'd done with Connor felt awful. But that wasn't what made my heart break. "No. It's not the sex." I sighed. "It's that I've hurt the people I love. I've let everyone down."

Spencer took back my resignation letter and ripped it in half. "I won't let you give up on something I know you still care about."

I took a deep breath to say something, but stopped. In fact, in that moment, I stopped *everything*. I stopped thinking about what the rest of the school thought. I stopped worrying about making Ms. Bee proud. I stopped thinking about Mike Domski's taunts and the look on my parents' faces as they trusted me. I turned off all that noise to ask myself one simple question:

What really matters here?

And it's by asking the question that I found the answer.

CHAPTER FORTY

I ran outside, hoping Autumn hadn't left school yet. I found her in the parking lot, sitting on the hood of her car with Marci and a bunch of other girls. They had the windows unrolled so they could hear her radio. She was happy, smiling.

I tried to be brave and put one foot in front of the other. It was like I was walking into a thick, heavy wind. Each step was labor. Everyone saw me approach. They got quiet and watched me struggle.

I stopped feet from the bumper. The headlights were on, and I squinted into the spotlight. The winter wind whipped my hair into my mouth when I opened it. I coughed, and the squeeze it put over my body didn't let go. I couldn't breathe, like the icy air was freezing me from the inside out.

"Natalie," Autumn said, springing to her feet. I heard the worry in her voice. She still cared for me, not that I deserved it. It felt like a dream, one too good for the nightmare life I'd been living. It was cruel, to have a moment of what our friendship once had been. A reminder of what I'd royally screwed up. I cried, because I didn't want to wake up.

Autumn didn't say good-bye to her friends. Or maybe she did, and I couldn't hear her over my sobbing. She put me in her car, and I watched them walk off in another direction. "I'm taking you home," Autumn announced, and climbed in the other side.

I cried the whole way.

Autumn helped me out of the car and walked me up the driveway. I leaned on her with all my weight, because I couldn't hold myself up. I mustered enough breath to say, "This is turning out to be a terrible apology," while Autumn found the spare key to our back door.

"It's okay," Autumn said. And the miracle was: As soon as she said it, things felt okay. Like I was getting where I needed to be.

When I'd run out of tears, Autumn and I sat on opposite ends of my bed, like it was a scale or a seesaw. I was still mustering up exactly what to say to her when she dropped a stone on my side.

"You never forgave me for what happened with Chad."

It wasn't so much the biting accusation of someone scorned as much as it was delivered in the calculated speak of a lawyer. An indisputable fact.

"I know," I said. "I was mad at you for getting hurt. I shouldn't have blamed you. It wasn't your fault."

Her bottom lip started to quiver. She took a deep breath and tried to compose herself. "When I went to see Chad that day in the locker room, there was this little voice in my head, telling me not to go. But I didn't listen to it. And that wasn't the first time I'd heard it, either. There were other times. *Lots* of other times. I can't explain it, but I think I knew deep down that Chad was no good. But I was too caught up in everything, how the fact that a boy liked me made me feel, that I thought I was in love with him."

"But Autumn, you couldn't have known that —"

"I've thought about this a million times. If I only would have listened to that voice, maybe none of that stuff would have happened to me. It was a lot of guilt to carry, on top of everything else. So I made a promise to myself that if I ever heard it again, I wouldn't shut it off. I think that's part of why I freaked out on you. Because that voice finally came back to me and told me that I was better than *Fish Sticks*. That I shouldn't hold myself back anymore. That I wasn't a bad person. And you were making me feel like a bad person, Natalie, when I was really just a girl who'd made a stupid mistake."

I nodded. "And I used that to keep you close to me. I had no other friends — and that's not your fault. It was mine. I've never been good at opening up to people."

"I know. Which makes what happened even more weird." She sighed. "I'm not saying this to be mean, but ... I can't believe you had sex with Connor Hughes."

I thought about Connor and his last words to me. How I could spin things any way I'd wanted. I could never understand how he always seemed sure of himself. But now I did. It was because Connor really did know what kind of person he was. He had no regrets because he always shot from his heart. He was the total opposite of someone like Chad Rivington. Or me.

"I wanted to," I told Autumn. It was the naked truth.

"Well, you're a smart girl, and I trust that you're going to make the right decisions for yourself."

"Yeah, because I'm the queen of right decisions."

Autumn took my hand. "You see, the best thing about wrong decisions is that they don't prevent you from making the right decisions later on. It's harder, but it's not impossible."

Time had taught her. And now she was teaching me.

CHAPTER FORTY-ONE

Did I regret having sex with Connor? A little. But it wasn't close to the earth-shattering regret I'd expected to feel. If anything, I regretted screwing up a beautiful moment because I was too messed up to see it as a good thing we'd done together, to see it as something shared by two people who really cared about each other.

The snow was falling steadily as I drove to Connor's house, tiny flakes like confetti. My windshield wipers swished across the glass like a metronome.

There was traffic all the way up the driveway. A man with a flashlight directed cars to a parking lot. Mostly minivans or SUVs, full of kids with knitted hats and scarves.

The Christmas tree farm was crawling with people. The parking guy directing cars, young girls dressed as elves, burly men with saws. The gift shop had Christmas music playing inside and a table set up outside where you could buy hot chocolate or hot apple cider to keep warm. There was even a reindeer in an enclosure that kids were feeding pellets.

Families waited for their turn to walk through the trees. I saw Connor leading a family of four through the snow. He only had on a thermal and a ski hat. I was wrapped up in my down parka and wondered how he wasn't freezing, until I saw one of the young boys pick out a tree. Connor grabbed his saw, dropped to his knees, and started to cut it down. He was there on the ground, working so hard. I watched as his muscles flexed. The tree fell against the snow and made the most wonderful sound. The family cheered. Connor tied some twine around the trunk and dragged it back through the snow for them.

He saw me then. I hoped he would come right over, but he looked away and kept dealing with the family.

He was not going to make this easy on me.

I walked over. "Can I please talk to you?" I asked.

"I can't right now, Sterling."

"Connor. Please."

He heard it in my voice, I'm sure. The pain.

"All right," he said.

He walked us over to the cider table, where his mother sat.

"Mom," he said, "I'm going to take a quick break."

She looked me over. I couldn't tell if she had recognized me from Thanksgiving morning. But she fixed me a cup of cider and Connor a cup of cocoa, a dollop of freshly made whipped cream on top.

Connor and I walked, our collective silence sad, layered over the sounds of families, of trees falling, of holiday music tinkling far away. The moon sat low in the sky, giving off barely enough light to see.

We didn't go to the shed. We didn't go to the house. We stayed in the woods, and I told him what I needed to tell him, unsure if it was what he needed to hear.

"I want to apologize for how I acted," I said. "I was afraid to get involved with you. I didn't want to admit that I liked you. I was afraid of how it would make me look."

"I can't be with someone who doesn't accept me for who I am."

"You have to understand, I'm new at this. And we both did things wrong. We got involved before we knew each other. I mean, I thought I knew you. But I didn't. Not really."

I tried to take his hand, only he wouldn't let me. He was shivering now, the cold setting in. "Do you regret what we did?" he asked. "Because that's been the worst part of this. Thinking you might hate me over what happened. I went through something like that once, with Bridget Roma. And it was terrible." His voice caught in his throat, and he tipped his head down. I saw tears in his eyes.

"Connor, that's not even close to what happened with us."

Even though I put every ounce of earnestness I could muster into my words, Connor still seemed uncertain. And he wasn't looking at me. He was focused on the footprints we'd left in the snow. "So where does that leave us now?" he asked.

"I want you to come to my portrait ceremony. As my date."

He didn't look up. "Really?"

"Really."

This time when I tried to take his hand, he let me. We stood like that, and for a brief moment, we were the center of the world.

I heard his mom calling for him, and he heard it, too.

"Go," I said.

"Are you sure?"

"Yeah. Go. I'll call you later."

It felt so easy, and even though it wouldn't always be, we were at least going to try.

◎ ◎ ◎

I didn't leave right away. I stayed in the woods. I heard the faint voices of other people. I felt the cold against my skin. But mostly, I was aware of my own breathing, my own thoughts, my own past, present, and future.

I realized then, and would have to keep realizing in all the years to come:

It didn't matter if I was the kind of girl who had sex, or the kind of girl who had her portrait on a wall in the library, or the kind of girl who got into the best college, or the kind of girl who didn't tell her parents everything, or the kind of girl who teachers loved.

I just needed to be okay with all the kinds of girl I was.

EPILOGUE

The library looked beautiful. Spencer had taken the lead and made herself the head of the decorating committee. She bought a nice tablecloth, cut cheese in perfect little squares, had the sparkling apple cider on ice. It was incredibly sweet, how proud she was of me. Like a little sister.

Everyone from student council showed up. My parents, Principal Hurley. I still caught some people whispering, but it didn't matter.

I found Connor near the portrait wall. He was alone now, but earlier he'd been animatedly discussing fantasy football picks with Martin and David and Dipak. It was nice to see, because things had definitely been strained within Connor's circle of friends. Those guys all still hung out together, playing Ping-Pong during lunch and drinking over at Bobby Doyle's house. But Connor hadn't talked to Mike since we decided to work things out. Mike hadn't talked to him, either.

I wasn't sure they'd ever speak again.

I had to believe their friendship would have ended eventually. Anyway, that's what Connor told me whenever I brought Mike up. Maybe Connor said it to make me feel better, or maybe he honestly believed it. But I learned that there had been other fights, other arguments before me. Just never any this big.

As much as I hated Mike, and would never forgive him for what he did to me and to my friends, I still felt the weight of a friendship ending because of the secrets I'd tried to keep. But Connor seemed at peace with how everything had played out. Ultimately, I needed to trust that Connor would do what was best for him. And he paid me the same courtesy, knowing I'd be hearing from colleges in a couple of weeks.

In the meantime, though, we simply loved each other.

"You look beautiful," Connor said, staring up at my portrait. He leaned in close and whispered, "And you can't see the hickey at all."

"Natalie? Could you come with me for a minute?" Ms. Bee appeared next to us, hands clasped in front of her.

I kissed him on the cheek, in front of everyone. "Be right back," I said.

Ms. Bee and I walked to the opposite side of the room without speaking.

It was hard for me to accept, how different our relationship suddenly was. After all, Ms. Bee wasn't my mother. She had no business forming an opinion on what I did or did not do in my personal life.

She'd handed me my college recommendation letter a week earlier. It was in a sealed envelope, as was standard practice. I worried for a second that Ms. Bee might have written something nasty about me. I think she must have seen it on my face, because she said, "Any college will be lucky to have you."

I knew she was still disappointed in me. And maybe it wasn't over Connor at all, but the way I'd been acting. Irresponsible. Flaky.

But all that had changed, now that Connor and I were out in the open. I was back on my game, and Ms. Bee would eventually have to notice.

Three older women stood near the shelf that held Ross Academy's old yearbooks. They had a bunch of them spread open on the table, poring over the pictures. Each of the ladies had name tags stuck to their dresses, but instead of names, they went by numbers.

Ms. Bee guided me forward. "May I present Natalie Sterling, number nine."

"Aren't you beautiful," number six said.

"We're so proud," number five said.

"Congratulations," number seven said.

I smiled my best smile. "Thank you so much for coming. I'm really honored."

"Are you kidding? This is so much fun for us old biddies." Number five squeezed my hand. "Getting to remember all the trouble we used to cause."

"None more so than number four right here," number seven said, pointing at Ms. Bee.

I'd never seen Ms. Bee blush before. Heck, I'd never seen Ms. Bee look anything other than perfectly poised. It was a huge relief.

Spencer flitted by with a bag of trash, collecting dirty napkins and empty cups. I grabbed her by the arm. "I want to introduce you all to Spencer Biddle, one of our freshmen representatives this year. I have no doubt that three years from now, her portrait will be up on the wall, too."

Spencer grinned. "You can call me Perfect Ten."

Ms. Bee almost choked.

Autumn came up and twirled me around. "I'm so proud of my best friend."

"Me too," I said. And we hugged each other as tightly as we could.

Of all the things to feel happy about, I was happiest that Autumn and I were friends again. No matter what the future held — new friends, new boyfriends, new directions — I knew we'd be in each other's lives forever. Change wasn't something to fear anymore. And even though my picture was on the wall, I didn't care so much about how I'd be remembered. So long as I never forgot.

Acknowledgements

Thanks to David Levithan and everyone at Scholastic, Rosemary Stimola, Nick Caruso, Brenna Vivian and the rest of the amazing Vivian clan, Emmy Widener, Lynn Weingarten, Caroline Hickey, Lisa Greenwald, Tara Altebrando, Brenna Heaps, Morgan Matson, Rachel Cohn, and Brian Carr. Also to Andrea Mondadori, for inviting me to the right place (her classroom) at exactly the right time (lunch).

HQ Young Adult
One Place. Many Stories

YOUNG
ADULT
H Q

The home of fun, contemporary
and meaningful Young Adult fiction.

Follow us online

 @HQYoungAdult

 @HQYoungAdult

 HQYoungAdult

 HQMusic2016